Fortune Telling

Fortune Telling

Short Stories

David Lynn

Carnegie Mellon University Press
Pittsburgh 1998

For W.F.S.

ACKNOWLEDGMENTS
The stories in this volume have appeared in the following magazines and journals: "Advert for Love," *Zoetrope*; "Rivalry," *TriQuarterly*; "Fortune Telling," *New England Review*; "Hypotenuse," *Boulevard*; "The Excuse," *Kansas Quarterly*; "Baiting," *Shenandoah*; "Wild Flowers," *Virginia Quarterly Review*; "Concert," *Present Tense*; "A Dancer," *Moment*; "Play," *The G.W. Review*; "When the Time is Right," *Present Tense*.

Library of Congress Card Catalog Number 97-0777971
ISBN 0-88748-283-X Pbk.
Copyright © 1998 by David Lynn
All Rights Reserved
Printed and Bound in the United States of America

10 9 8 7 6 5 4 3 2 1

CONTENTS

FORTUNE TELLING / 9

WILD FLOWERS / 31

HYPOTENUSE / 49

RIVALRY / 55

CONCERT / 67

ADVERT FOR LOVE / 83

BAITING / 91

A DANCER / 103

HARD FEELINGS / 119

THE EXCUSE / 133

PLAY / 149

WHEN THE TIME IS RIGHT / 169

RECOLLECTIONS / 189

THE LAKESHORE LIMITED / 209

Fortune Telling

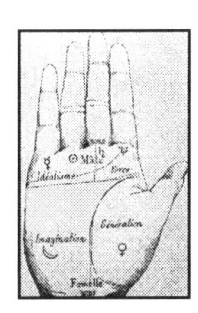

Perpendicular to the highway north of town and directly opposite the new GE plant stood the sign: Mme. Sosostra, Palm Reader, Fortune Teller. And of course, an erect palm in red. Behind it a tidy prefab cottage perched on the lip of the highway. Passing traffic had strewn the porch with sand and stray bits of gravel.

I accompanied Sara to the steps where she turned me back with a smile and a raised palm of her own. Inside the screen door two young children were playing with matchbox cars on the floor, cartoons flashing on the tv behind them. A heavy woman in a red smock hurried from the back as if she'd intuited our arrival. Stepping over the children, she pushed the screen open with one hand. I retreated to wait in Sara's car.

We'd driven hers because, as I explained when she called—out of the blue—my own car was in the shop. "That's okay," she said. "The point isn't for you to chauffeur me. Ten minutes and I'll pick you up?"

"Fine by me," I said. "But where to?"

"It's only because Joseph refuses. And I thought I could talk you into it."

"I guess I'm flattered."

"You won't laugh, Peter. Promise?" She hesitated before rushing ahead. "See, I'm having my palm read. I've wanted to for ages but never got up the nerve." She sounded embarrassed and breathless and determined. "You don't do it for real, but for fun. Like shooting miniature golf. This woman's supposed to be spooky-good."

Watching for her car, I dragged a rocking chair across the battered front porch of the farmhouse I was rehabbing.

Why choose me? I wondered. What did she have in mind?

Not that I wasn't pleased.

Sara Burnwell and I always had a good time when we were thrown together at a picnic or ballgame. We'd joke, agreeing with an arched eye over bowls of chili at someone else's silliness or pomposity. But as I watched for a plume of dust along the gravel road it occurred to me that I'd never once been alone with Sara for more than two minutes. There'd never been the opportunity or the reason.

After all, I knew her only because Joe and I played softball on the same team during the summer. Poker once a month in winter.

Ours was a hodge-podge group of friends. We liked to play ball, liked pizza and beer as rewards for the red dust in eyes and nostrils and under nails, for the strawberry hip scrapes earned sliding into base on a rocky field. Liked most of all, perhaps, the time spent with each other, guys we didn't work with, didn't even see except by chance on the street. Unless we made the reason—a game, a barbecue, one of those chili-cookoffs.

Short, stocky, with powerful shoulders and a grin flashing out from his black beard, Joe Burnwell was astonishingly graceful. He'd glide toward a hard ground ball, gather it up even while beginning his spin round in the air, and launch it towards first base with the off-balance balance of a dancer, never losing the cigarette in his mouth or his mathematician's absolute concentration on the arc of the ball.

I can picture him with his students, puzzling out some mathematial conjecture with that same concentration. But I *see* him silently tracking the flow of cards in a seven-card game, absently patting the top of his head with one hand. Or he'd be hunched over a conversation in a living-room corner, whether about the major league standings or the latest outrage by some university dean. A couple of our other friends gathered close.

Meanwhile, him in that corner, I'm sipping on a beer and trying to cool down from my latest row with Donna—the woman I'd been seeing for nearly two years—probably because she'd refused, again, to come along to the party. "Pretend I'm there," she'd say. "It's always the same anyway. Same people, same conversations. I've got better things to do than stand around with the girls chatting about someone else's kids. Besides, the kiln's fired and I've got orders to deliver."

Other than brushing past the little knots of conversation for the sake of diplomacy, Sara Burnwell wouldn't be standing around with the girls either. An inch or two taller than her husband, she was very thin, so thin that even her best clothes would hang at oblique angles like hand-me-downs. She'd skirt along the edge of the gathering, plastic cup in hand, squinting with wry pleasure at all the fuss of a party that didn't quite include her. She dipped gingerly in and out of the chat with a quick irony that protected her.

To our weekend softball games Sara would sometimes bring one of the kids the county assigned her. Some were battered or abused, some were delinquent in a simple old-fashioned way. But several—I remember one, a tough-looking girl of twelve, hair bleached a greenish yellow, nervous hands that picked and picked—several of them shared a certain look as they perched in the stands, a skittishness, as if a high whistle no one else could make out was tingling in the air. And Sara, the social worker responsible for them, she shared that look—she seemed to hear the same distant music, and the listening kept her a little bit apart from the rest of us.

The others in that crowd never seemed to mind or even to catch Sara's delicate reserve. Smile on her face, cup in her hand, she'd be standing ever so slightly aside while her husband flipped burgers and recounted impossible stories from his Vietnam stint in military intelligence. Drunken generals and hookers mistaken as girls or mistaken as boys. Booby-trapped corpses that exploded from their own gas. A circle of friends, men and women, would be writhing with laughter as Joe, deadpan, shared these tales.

Because I was often on my own—Donna sealed away in her damn pottery studio—I'd be separate too without wanting to be. That may be why I was the one who recognized the arm's length at which Sara held us all. From time to time we, she and I, acknowledged the secret with a glance. She'd be a little bit angry with me for noticing, a little bit grateful.

"You can't tell anyone I made you do this," she said as she climbed back into the car at Madame Sosostra's. Her face was lightly flushed and she released her hair with a shake from a tortoise-shell clip.

"Who's to tell?" I said.

"I don't know if she's a fortune teller or a mind reader, but it's pretty unnerving. More than I expected anyway."

"Yeah? What kind of news is she predicting? Remember, if there's loot I claim a share."

For a moment she seemed not to be listening, or listening again only to that distant music of hers. Suddenly she looked at me, cocked her head, made a face. "Trust me—you'll be the first millionaire I create." Her sarcasm mocked Madame Sosostra, me, not least herself.

She noticed something out the window and I sensed another abrupt switch in mood. "I can't really tell you anything," Sara said. "She's sworn me to secrecy. Besides," this she flung offhand, "if there's anything good, telling'll only spoil it."

Only in that instant did I become uncomfortable. Until then this all had been a playful self-indulgence, a toying with superstition for the fun of it, not believing even while observing the rule. Like a baseball coach stepping across the foul line. Yet some shadow of an ache in her voice hinted that, whatever trust she placed in Madame Sosostra's special gifts, she'd more on her mind than the whim to decipher a future mapped in her own palm.

"So what now?" I asked. "Drop me home? Or we can find a cup of coffee somewhere."

She pushed a hand through her hair and arched her neck with a deep breath, and suddenly it was just Sara Burnwell again. "Sure," she said. "This is Joseph's night for crunching numbers in his office, so I'm free for a while yet. Though I'm not sure coffee's what I want this late."

✳

It's only now, in telling the story, that I'm aware of how predictable this part seems. It didn't feel that way in the early summer evening. Or maybe I was blind. It may be there's a momentum to our actions, to the particular paths we're on, that we aren't entirely aware of or don't dare trust at the time. Not to mention the difficulty of making out unexpected branches in the path ahead.

For lack of any better notion, we wound up back at my farmhouse. Most of my furniture was in storage and the living room was all but bare. So we settled next to each other on an old rug, sipping glasses of cold wine. It was dangerous. It was exciting. I was certainly aware of momentum now. This woman was a mystery. What did she want? What was I supposed to do? Heaven knows what we talked about.

My hand brushed hers, or hers mine, as I poured another glass. Joking around—always safe with irony—I lifted her hand and kissed it like a dramatic cavalier.

Sara rose onto her knees and stared crossly at me. Leaning forward awkwardly, she placed her hands on either side of my face and tugged me towards her. We fumbled an off-balance kiss against each other and fell apart once more, panting, as if the joining had been deeper, longer.

"I'm surprised," I murmured at last. "But I've wanted to do that for a long time." That was true, though I'd just discovered it.

Her hair had fallen across her face. She was shaking her head quizzically. "I think about you a lot, Peter. Lately, it's hard thinking about anything else, even when I'm with Joseph."

Again, abruptly, I was uncertain, uncomfortable. I didn't much want to hear about Joseph. And I was as startled by her declaration as pleased. I'd never sensed any such intensity before, nothing beyond an occasional tame flirtation.

"Any of this to do with your fortune teller? How come you took me along?"

She flashed her teeth in a quick smile. "It's absolutely true what I said—Joseph refused to go. But I wanted you along. And she spotted it immediately. She knew you weren't my husband."

"So come on, what the hell'd she predict?"

Sara laughed a naughty laugh. "I told you—I can't tell you. It was about other things too. But *I* predict this isn't the last." She leaned forward and kissed me again even as she was rolling onto her knees and rising. "I've got to get home."

Nodding, I leaned back on an arm.

As it happened, the next evening we had a softball game. But Sara wasn't in the stands, and it was anybody's guess (my guess) when I'd see her again. Donna was to meet me after the game for a quick bite and a film.

The umpire was a few minutes late, so we had time to warm up. As I was lacing my cleats, Joe Burnwell finished a smoke and dug a couple of balls out of the duffel bag. We trotted away from the bench together. Heading towards second base, he flipped me one of the balls with a grin. It was the last thing I needed.

A year earlier, maybe a year and a half, Joe had dropped by my office. "Hey, Pete—you busy?" I glanced up as he stood tapping at the doorframe. He looked rumpled and lost in a jacket, loose tie, and jeans.

In fact I *was* busy. Our agency was supposed to have a model of the town's new recreation center on display in two days. But I was so surprised to see Joseph downtown in the middle of the week that I waved him in.

"Nah," he said, shaking his head. "Don't let me bother you. Unless you've got a minute?"

I gathered he wanted me to come with him. "Sure," I said.

Once outside, however, Joe was at a loss, didn't even seem to know where he was. It was a warm afternoon, the sun soaking the brick pavement and radiating heat. I tugged him towards a cafe. We slipped into a cool booth in back.

His dark hair was combed, his beard neat and trim, but his skin looked clammy and his eyes were red-rimmed. I waited, asking nothing.

"Someone's died," he murmured at last. "Someone I knew. A friend called me last night at the office to let me know."

"I'm sorry," I said because there was nothing else to say.

"Margaret—she's the one who's died—she's the only other woman I ever lived with. For two years almost, while I was at school up in Rochester." He sat there and shook his head and stared in amazement. "Sara knows about all that of course. But not that we almost had a kid. Even had names ready to go. But then we lost it—Margaret fell—

and everything kind of collapsed. The pieces just wouldn't fit again."

I nodded silently and shifted an empty coffee cup in my hands.

"How could I not know? How could she not at least let me know?" he demanded, patting the table softly so that he didn't have to slam it. "She's had cancer—she had cancer—for over a year. Our friend said it was about as bad as it gets, just slowly eating away at Margaret until there wasn't enough left to be worth the eating."

Joe and I sat there and talked or didn't talk until the dinner crowd was crowding for tables, and by then it was time for him to go home to Sara anyway.

Why did he come to *me*? Maybe because we weren't close friends but weren't strangers either. Maybe because a past that couldn't be included in the present had intruded there anyway and couldn't be swept away without some kind of acknowledgment.

We weren't really closer for it afterwards, not in any overt way. He never mentioned it again, nor did I. But it meant something to me. Like a secret gift.

So Joseph was fielding grounders at second base, dancing to his right, lunging left for the ball, caught up in the pleasure of the rhythms, the calculated intercessions of his glove. Deep in the outfield I was shagging flies, still dazed from Sara's revelations of the night before and my own discovery of desire. Not to mention dazed from a long afternoon on-site translating blueprints to guys with bulldozers.

What did I owe Joseph?

We'd been friendly for three or four years now. One afternoon's confidences aside, were we friends? I'd always had plenty of good will towards him. I spent about as much time with him, in company with others of course, as with most anyone outside the office, not including Donna.

And Donna? True to her artist's persona her attitude towards our relationship—such as it was—qualified as free-form. Betrayal seemed too grand a word for anything that might concern her, or so I was willing to believe.

Nor did I worry about adultery as such. That was Sara's business (and Joseph's), not a larger social sin that bruised my shoulders.

But *friendship*. A single confession in the cafe nudged aside once more, the fact is I'd never had much to say to Joseph. Maybe it was the professor in him, but he was always on stage, performing, entertaining. Not to the point of being obnoxious but not inviting intimacy either. For all that good will between us, he and I had never really managed anything *more* than good will. What kind of bond was that? What responsibilities trailed along?

At the plate, our captain Jamie Roth swung his bat and the ball soared, chased by an unearthly aluminum *ping*. I settled under the long fly with the faint hitch of breath that never doesn't come before the ball strikes your glove.

✳

Later that week Sara called and we arranged to meet for a stroll in a small park near Court Square. From my office window I spotted her on the street, and I was on the sidewalk before she crossed over. Instead of hurrying directly towards each other, we played it coy, teasing along, and angled separately for the head of the path into the park. Hands clasped behind her back, Sara half-skipped ahead in her flat shoes and summer print dress. She refused to glance my way.

I reached the path first and turned in just ahead of her beside a great bank of flowering azaleas. She caught me by the sleeve. "Hi," she said, giving me a peck on the cheek as if it were the most natural thing in the world, then falling into step alongside, eyes on her shoes, hands behind her back again, an impish smile on her lips.

An echo of her cologne lingered on my skin and struck me drunk in exact proportion to its faintness. It measured the uncertainty not only of what was to come but of what I wanted to. We strolled openly as if courting observation as well as each other. To see us, we might have been discussing business, provider and client; we might have been casual friends who'd bumped into each other; we might have been lovers. I was surprised at the excitement gathering and tightening along the sinews in my chest and arms and throat. Every second or third step we'd brush and bump against each other, stumbling ever so slightly.

As we turned onto another path she drew away almost imperceptibly, absorbed in reflection. "I've been thinking about it." Her head was tucked down, studying the white gravel. (A client explaining her decision on colors.) "I know it's all just happened, or hasn't even happened yet. But there's something special between us, Peter. Isn't there? You know there is. And I'm afraid if we don't snatch it up we may lose it." She paused. (No, not eggshell, maybe a delicate blue . . . .) "I think we ought to make love. We ought to be lovers."

And I'm nodding sagely, oh yes, taking counsel of her wishes.

If only we weren't so responsible—if I hadn't had meetings that afternoon, she clients of her own, more of those children to rescue from parents, each other, themselves. If only we'd rushed away that very moment to one of the inns nestled in the mountains and devoured each other, we might have been able to enjoy a simple straightforward fling and left it at that.

✳

Joe did have a private hobby. Back in college he'd earned his wings in ROTC, and once a week or so he rented a small plane to take out on his own. These late-afternoon or evening flights were the times that Sara and I stole away by ourselves. What with the price of a hired plane, it never gave us very long. We'd drive out into the country, as high into the fringe of mountains as time allowed. Every now and then I sensed Joseph tracking somewhere in the sky above us, though we never spotted the plane. Still, he'd be there over my shoulder, unseen and unforgotten.

We didn't spend the entire time actually driving, of course. Like a couple of teenagers we'd pull off the road into a layby or an overgrown track, grabbing urgently at each other, wrestling and clutching to beat the time back. Again and again I was startled by her soft lips as I kissed them, by her full breasts as I cupped them—she was so light in my arms otherwise, a bundle of bones that couldn't be as frail as they seemed.

Things got pretty hot. But truth is we never quite hit combustion. We seemed to lack the spark for that leap. Or I did. There'd be a tiny line of sweat across Sara's lip or a bead at her temples. She'd draw back from my arms, breathing hard, and not quite look at me, but stare out through the window even if there was nothing to see but branches or rock, not seeing anything, listening to her silent music, and waiting for me. After that first declaration in the park of what she thought we ought to do, she never mentioned it directly again.

One evening, as the scent of pine awakened about us like night birds and blossomed into a gauzy blue dusk, Sara and I held each other like an old married couple with no hurry, no urgency to complete what hadn't yet happened. We were whispering this and that, sharing thoughts and secrets as they occurred to us. We were great talkers that summer. I talked because I didn't want to discover why I was content not to push farther with her—as I had every intention of doing, every fantasy of fulfilling, as long as the two of us weren't actually jammed together with the passenger seat tilted all the way back. Sara talked, I came to realize, because she needed to, more perhaps than she needed all the rest.

"And besides, he wants kids," she was saying.

I nodded, drowsy, half-listening, spellbound by the warmth of our bodies and the smell of the pines.

"You aren't paying a damn's worth of attention," she snapped, and jabbed me with an elbow.

"Ouch—all right, all right." Contritely as the darkness allowed, I turned more fully to her.

"Joseph wants kids. And these doctors are predicting I can't have any."

"You've gone to more than one?"

"I've gone to a bunch."

I shrugged. "What about adopting?"

"It isn't the same—they wouldn't really be his." Her voice hadn't risen so much as swooped from casual storytelling to a tight-throated murmur.

"He's said that?"

She didn't quite shrug. She looked away.

"Wait, just wait," I said. "Does he know what the doctors say?"

She hesitated, shook her head, bit her lip. "He'll leave me when he finds out. Not that he'd admit it, even to himself. And it wouldn't be right away of course. But I know him. And his family. Kids are too important. He'll find an excuse to leave." Rather than stiffening or pulling away, she nestled deeper into my arms.

I nuzzled and nipped at her ear. "What the hell are you doing with me?" I whispered.

She pinched a finger's worth of flesh through my shirt. "You, you're the most terrific. You're my secret, my friend."

It's not that I didn't believe her, though the suspicion nagged that I was conveniently at hand for some purpose still unspoken. Yet that furtive little smile she let me glimpse, including me in her pain and fears, was a solid blow to the chest, a thump that left a hollow ache of yearning more profound than anything I'd yet felt. An echo lingered in the bone and I seemed at last to be hearing that secret music of hers.

That's when the love would have happened, she and I rising to each other. Except that our time was up. Somewhere in the darkness overhead an airplane was soaring towards home, and Sara had to track a different path towards the same center, two poles of a compass rushing together. Each time necessity reaffirmed the pivot of that compass, I became extraneous. In front of the dark house Sara hesitated and turned back. She leaned through the driver's window and kissed me in the public darkness of their street.

*

Sara was busy with her wayward children; I was busy; Joseph wasn't flying. And so it was a good ten days before I saw her again. Ten days to take stock, and what did I discover? That I missed Sara, found myself thinking of her on the flimsiest associations, would have admitted outright (to myself) that I loved her, if not for a deep wariness of that word.

The fact that Joseph also loved her was a hinge to the matter over which I had no control. Either he cared enough for her so that children finally didn't matter, (a possibility I hardly credited, taking refuge in her sworn certainty), or siring his own offspring was part of some ineluctable mathematical projection more potent than love.

The fact that she loved him . . . . I did my best to ignore that side of it. For that's what I'd also glimpsed in the dusk of the mountains. That she still loved him. That regardless of whatever she felt for me, she'd stumbled my way not out of boredom or distaste or merely because she wanted someone prepared to catch her should he cast her off, but because she was creating, out of love, a ready escape for *him*. A reason (were we discovered) by which he could leave without feeling guilty or responsible. Did I love her enough to be playing in that league?

※

Wonder of wonder, Donna was actually eager to go to the late-summer barbecue at Jamie Roth's house, his annual end of season bash. When I pulled up to her rambling studio, she was waiting in the door, wearing a bright green dress loose in the skirt and tight across her chest. A silk scarf she'd printed by hand bound her red hair in a long pony-tail.

"Hello Stranger," she called with a wry smile. She skipped down the steps, and her eagerness, her dress, the smile she was wearing all accused me of neglect. For once she couldn't complain that I demanded too much.

"A party is just what I need—the timing's perfect," she said, kissing me hello. "Can you believe that elementary school painting lessons start up again next week?"

I kissed her. I knew perfectly well why I'd been, why I was attracted to this woman, with her high brow and smallish mouth. Her excitement caught me up.

Yet within a few moments as we drove a familiar tension gathered in the car. Or rather, I was the one who grew tense. Donna turned on the radio and searched for music. And I sat there wondering whether her sarcasm might be conjured this evening—by someone's chatter about sports or recent movies, by gossip about university politics or small-town infidelities. The casual intimacy we'd earned over two years seemed a strange burden. And what, what in the whole world would she and I manufacture to talk about when, in truth, I had nothing to say?

"You're a thousand miles away, aren't you?" she said, startling me. Puzzled more than suspicious, a furrow above her eyes represented still another accusation.

The afternoon had already begun its bleed into late-summer twilight when we arrived. Jamie was barbecuing chicken on a brace of grills in the drive. (He never allowed the rose garden in back, his pride and joy, to be defiled by smoke and fire.) "Hello," we cried from the curb as if very far away. He was wiping a long fork on his apron and he saluted, fork to Red Sox cap, sweat beading beatifically across his face.

With a wave at him we slipped into Kara Roth's large kitchen. Most of the crowd was already gathered in force. Behind them, a row of high windows opened out onto the garden. That's where I spotted Joseph wandering alone, hands in his pockets, cigarette in his mouth. From island to island of roses he drifted, stopping at last in front of an enormous old-fashioned rose bush, its progeny of delicate buds and vines and blown blossoms backed against a lattice. He didn't seem unhappy or lonely, merely thoughtful, as if he were off by himself without a friend for miles. Watching him through the windows, *I* was the one who felt a stab of loneliness.

For all that, it surprised me that he wasn't in here with us. Smoke or no smoke, it wasn't like Joe. And as I watched him, what had seemed mere thoughtfulness darkened its hue, became a burden that rounded his shoulders, that bowed his head. He seemed smaller, more vulnerable as he took a long last drag at his cigarette and flicked it towards a mulch heap.

The trail of dying smoke caught me up in a transformation that very moment, not in the figure before me but in my own capacity to see. Suspicion drew my head up. Behind me the kitchen was curling itself around a single conversation in multiple registers. Just then the crowd parted far enough for Donna to slip through. She was carrying two glasses of wine. For an instant I stared at her in confusion and alarm. I'd forgotten entirely that she was here, half expected a caustic *J'accuse* from her lips. "I'm surprised you didn't mention it," she said sharply.

"Mention?"

"About the Burnwells." She looked at me for confirmation. Of what? Was that scorn in her eyes? Did she suspect after all?

"You haven't heard? Some university in Illinois just made Joseph an offer he can't refuse."

I accepted a glass and sipped at it, terribly proud of my calm, triumphant that I'd guessed something was up before--at least slightly before--being slapped with it. "Isn't it awfully late for that?" I said as if she'd know, flaunting my cold-blooded control. "Aren't classes about to begin?"

"Don't ask me," she said with a shrug. "But I'll miss him. Joseph's about the only one of this bunch who's always good for a laugh or an argument."

By now a rhythm had established itself to the stages of my enlightenment, and I was hardly startled to glance up and discover Sara on the threshold to the living room. Only for that instant did she stare directly at me, her eyes flat, her lips pressed thin. Then she disappeared again into the crowd.

In mind and spirit I chased her for the rest of the evening. But for once chance didn't seem inclined to shuffle the two of us together. Donna was attentive. She was, of all ironies, quite delighted to be here. Nor did the party thin out as night deepened. It seemed that everyone wanted to cling to this last flourish of summer. Bottles of wine appeared beaded with moisture along their cold flanks. Jamie hoisted his stereo speakers into those tall kitchen windows and flung old blues into the garden. Candles flickered in bowls on the grass. Soon the cottage was all but deserted as everyone sought the night air. Alone no longer, Joseph sat on the grass with his knees drawn up as he recounted the amazing developments of the past couple of weeks, encircled by friends eager to learn more and lament.

My turn to fetch refills from the kitchen. I was balancing a precarious triangle of glasses when Sara appeared in the door and drew me aside. A moment was all we had, but I couldn't think of anything to say. I wanted to shout at her, and couldn't. I wanted to drop the glasses, gather her in my arms, kiss her, and couldn't.

"Joseph's no fool," she said as if we were already well launched. "I couldn't be thinking of you all the time and not have him guess."

"Does he know?" I hissed more harshly than I'd intended.

"Nothing specific. Not who. Or even if, for sure." She glanced away over my shoulder, a distant anger already cooling in her eyes. "And anyway Peter, you've been a perfect gentleman. Nothing's really happened, has it?"

"Nothing's happened?"

She cut me off as if I hadn't made a sound. "But he's guessed something or heard rumors." She lifted two of the glasses from my hands and carried them to the counter. "Did you know they were courting him last year? Brought him out to Illinois to give a paper. But he wasn't interested. Not then." She sounded matter-of-fact as she poured the wine.

"Ten days ago Joe calls to see if something might still be possible, even a visiting slot for now. Not that he tells me. Day before yesterday he lets me in on the secret. Their dean's created a new slot just for him. Of course my job's no problem. There're kids for a social worker most anywhere."

There was a pause for a sigh, but she didn't sigh. Looking at me again, she searched my eyes, flicking from one to the other. "You know what's funny?—my fortune teller didn't let on about this. She was pretty hot on the good, not so hot on the bad."

"You don't have to go."

She smiled and put a hand on my arm as if I'd said the right thing and was just precious for it. But as she looked at me a frown gathered. "You're really squeamish about him knowing, aren't you?"

"You've got a job here," was all I could muster. "Those kids depend on you." I inched closer and held out the third glass for her to fill. "I'm not ready to lose you, not like this." That, at least, was true.

"It's all happening so fast," she said, again as if I hadn't spoken. "We're supposed to be packed for the movers in nine days."

I wanted to shout at her, and didn't. I wanted to drop the glasses, gather her in my arms, kiss her, and didn't. "That's it then? You're going for sure?"

She shrugged and for the first time she let me spy the confusion and ache in her eyes. "I don't know—I don't know. But I've got to see you before."

"God, yes," I said.

*

Where can one flee in a small town for absolute privacy in the middle of the day, especially when the business at hand is something more than a quick screw? Where is one least likely to run into friends and acquaintances? Sara and I arranged to meet at the famous estate of an early President, up in the hills above town. We'd take refuge in the swirl of tourists.

Shrieking babies and clicking cameras did indeed create a blizzard of noise as we trudged up from the parking lot alongside a busload of visitors. To blend in, Sara had thought to bring along a camera. We went so far as to hold hands, though that was probably an unnecessary risk.

As the visitors streamed up to the house, the two of us swerved aside and wandered into the relative peace of the gardens. Beyond the slave quarters a tall stand of boxwood opened like a magic cabinet onto a dark clearing. It was cooler here and quieter. The rest of the world dropped entirely away. But we were vulnerable to invasion at any moment, to being flushed into the open, and that increased the urgency we would have felt in any event. Letting the camera tumble onto the grass, Sara swung round without letting go of my hand, reached up and tugged my head down for a quick fierce kiss.

"I don't know how many more of those I get," she murmured.

A grief sharper than I expected wrenched my throat and chest. Yet there was an undeniable flush of relief as well. I didn't trust myself to speak. I didn't want to loathe myself later for hypocrisy or easy cliche. Instead I slipped my arms around her waist and drew her close for a longer kiss.

At last she twisted her face to the side and leaned against me. "I haven't stopped thinking about you for a second. That's what's so scary." I felt the warmth of her breath through my shirt.

"That sounds like a crazy reason for leaving," I murmured.

"Don't you see, it's the craziness that scares me. Obsessions I can deal with when it's the kids they send me, but my own—"

"That makes it a hell of a lot easier for me."

"Oh, don't be angry. There's no time for that. You're lovely and sweet and I do love you."

A couple months worth of frustration welled like bile I couldn't swallow back. "If you're so goddam sure that sooner or later Joseph will disappear anyway, why the hell are you following him now?" The imminence of actually losing her had me arguing more passionately than I'd intended, than I had any right to do.

She shrugged and turned her head. "Maybe it has to be his choice. I can't do it on my own."

"You've done a damn fine job so far."

Her eyes flashed. "And you've made it so easy, haven't you? You've been a prince. Nothing to be ashamed of. Not you."

She was panting lightly. "You've left the worst to me over and over again. No, you haven't really betrayed your friend Joseph, have you? Isn't that it, Peter? You've had it both ways—teasing the danger with me and always keeping one foot safe." She snorted. "The bunch of you—with your little-boy games. Making believe you're pals, buddies. You don't have a clue about friends, or about love."

The taste of her accusations was bitter, jammed like a brass bit between my teeth. Without moving an inch, Sara left me behind, drifted miles away. And that sharp bit—the sour brass of my own failure suddenly come home—it kept me from reaching towards her even as I longed to. Instead, something collapsing, I turned aside and retrieved her camera from the ground. Stepping back I snapped her once, twice, and slipped aside for a better angle. As I collected souvenirs with each flash, the future came a little clearer.

All the talk behind us now, Sara darted forward and snatched the camera away. She got two clear shots at me before an older couple discovered the little clearing.

"Hello," I shouted too loudly. "Do us a favor, would you?"

Glad to oblige, the old man fumbled stiff fingers over the camera and aimed it at the pair of us while his wife grinned on.

Wild Flowers

Etta Bloch tended her memories. Tended her husband Manny and their son Jake like flowers, though not to grow and blossom—simply to remain fresh and alive in her mind. They were her responsibility, and by her attentions she kept them from wilting, from fading as long as she did.

This was nothing she'd set her mind to at first. How could she not think of her boy, after all—cut off like that at twenty-nine, his face cut up so by the glass and the phone pole that the undertakers could hardly make him decent?

For weeks that was all she could see, his face in the hospital (it had only been a formality for the rescue squad to carry him there) and then, stitched along the great flap that had torn loose along the line of his jaw and up round his ear and just under his eye, in the casket that only she and Manny peeked into to say goodbye.

For weeks afterwards Etta spied her son out of the corner of her eye and everywhere she turned. Always in these quickest of glimpses Jake'd be staring back at her out of that poor torn face, sometimes with one of his mischievous grins or about to whistle, (everyone knew him for his whistle—he was a wonderful whistler), sometimes round-eye scared. And there'd be salt on her lips while she was still trying to keep her limbs from shaking, her chest from collapsing. What would Manny do if she collapsed?

Jake's face in the casket was the only thing she allowed herself to forget. Until she could manage to do so, however—and it was a long time—the jagged smile on his cold lips stood between her and the real memories, the ones from when he was a boy especially, and turned them into false dreams.

One morning while she was fixing breakfast, Etta heard Manny sigh above the burbling of the oatmeal pot. "What'd you say?" she called. Funny she should hear it in the kitchen. She thought so then, but he didn't say anything more. If he was thinking about Jake, well, she was curious—he never, ever, spoke about their son, which meant she had to do the talking for them both, or do none at all. On the other hand, she acknowledged with a flick of the ladle, what point was there in knowing what had Manny sighing—it would probably only make those bad memories of hers flare up but good.

With the back of her ladle she shaped the oatmeal into an island, around which he'd pour skim milk. Somehow the thought that she shouldn't have been able to hear him sigh flattened the surprise as she backed through the swinging door and discovered Manny slumped at his place. His cheek was resting on one arm, as if he were stealing a quick nap while she got ready for work at Dr. Wilder's office.

Carefully Etta set the bowl down and hurried back to the phone in the kitchen. She could count on the town's rescue squad arriving in under five minutes, but she knew already that time didn't matter--they could take their time. Returning to the table, she slipped onto her own seat and rested her head on her arm and stared at Manny, who was smiling in his sleep, nothing crooked to his mouth.

It seemed that Sarah Abrams arrived before the rescue squad. Though that wasn't possible, was it? Perhaps Etta had called her too?—She didn't have the strength to recall. Her arms and tongue were leaden. She felt heavy, too heavy even to think. For that she was grateful.

While Etta sat dazed in her chair, desperately trying to recall Manny's face, Sarah was puttering about. Arranging things on the phone, picking out Manny's dark suit to take to the funeral home. Sometime after ten, Harry Abrams, Sarah's husband, walked through the screen door—it was as soon as he could close his second-hand furniture shop and hurry on over. Harry was wearing his rumpled corduroy jacket and smelling of pipe smoke. It was Harry who called the rabbi in Richmond.

By afternoon the small clapboard bungalow was buzzing. Gladys Shapiro brought the first load of food—a sponge cake, smoked trout from up on the mountain, hushpuppies—and having seen these provisions safely into the fridge and straightened her wig, Gladys seized a plastic pail and a rag and set to cleaning. No one was paying any attention to Etta, not for the time being, except to set a mug of tea in front of her and to replace it in due course with another.

In the early evening it was Harry again who took her hand. "It's time we went on over," he whispered and drew her up out of her chair. Then they were in Harry's ancient Studebaker. Then they were at the funeral home, Harry handing her over to Mordecai Smith.

"Thank God he felt nothing," Mordi said.

Etta stared at him blankly.

"Do you want to see him now, before the others arrive?" he asked. "We'll have to close the casket by then."

She shook her head. But he took her hand, coaxed her to sit down in his office for a few moments, and, without asking a second time, led her to a small curtained area in back.

He all but shooed her forward to the casket. "I'll leave you for a few minutes—as long as you like, Etta."

Oh, but she fooled him. She walked five paces towards that casket with her eyes closed. Listened to what Mordi said and stood there in the middle of the little room with her eyes closed. She didn't want to see whatever was in the casket. She'd learned her lesson with Jake. She wanted to be able to remember Manny right off, not be blocked by how they'd posed him.

Dressing him, of all things, in that stylish mail-order suit she'd made him buy years before—a suit with a pinstripe, a suit he'd laughed at even though he knew it hurt her feelings, a suit he'd worn a first time to take her out for her birthday, and once again five years later for Jake, and then never again. What use had he for such a suit?

※

Late on this Friday afternoon, like every other business day, Etta drew out the files of Dr. Wilder's scheduled patients for the next day (Saturday a.m. only), ticking a pencil in the upper right hand corner for those who hadn't had their teeth x-rayed in two years. She tidied-up a bit for the maid, and double-checked that the water was turned off in the bowls by Dr. Wilder's two chairs. Her coat and scarf off the hanger, a flick to the lights, and she trotted silently in her white shoes down to the street just in time to catch Hoke Perkins' 5:10 Locust Avenue bus.

There wasn't a seat, not at this hour, but Etta wasn't going far, and she squeezed out a place for herself in the aisle between Mr. Klagholz, who owned two Hallmark shops, and Virginia Watley, poor dear, who was having some pretty bad trouble with her gums (she smiled distractedly at Etta, her lips pressed tight together).

The bus cut across the older part of town, skirting Court Square on its way out to the new shopping mall and subdivisions. But it was only down the hill from the old courthouse that

Hoke Perkins made a special stop in the middle of the block for Etta—she didn't even have to ring the bell. From the rear door she gave him a quick little wave in his mirror and all but jumped down, eager for her favorite evening of the week.

Smiling to herself, excited, Etta opened the door of the bungalow, stepped across the threshold, and turned up the thermostat—the house was chilly after the long cool day. She wasn't thinking about Manny or Jake. No, no, that wouldn't do, not yet. They'd simply have to wait. She sighed at the thought—it was she who had to wait, and the anticipation, the flirting with the pleasure to come, was delicious.

Instead of cleaning the house on weekends as in the old days, she'd taken to sweeping and washing and polishing on Thursday night with the tv turned up loud. And last night—such a productive evening, so much accomplished—she'd also made a fresh chicken casserole (with a good dollop of sweet German wine) all ready to slip in the oven now. Into the oven it went, and a good dollop of French bath oils she poured into the bathtub as it filled with hot, hot water.

She was humming something from the FM channel that Dr Wilder played in the office all day. It was an old, pretty song, one of those songs by Henry Mancini or someone like that. She was humming as she took off her new uniform—nearly new, anyway. She'd given this style a try since the material was supposed to be easy to clean. But what she'd discovered was that the dress grew awfully hot during the day, and now the collar was already yellowing and they said you shouldn't use bleach on this space-age material.

This was the reward, this the glory as she eased slowly, carefully into the almost-too-hot water. Its surface shimmered with delicate colors from the bathoils that protected her skin, (always prone to drying out and to sprouting patches of psoriasis, especially as the weather grew colder this time of year). And the glint of the water smoothed and disguised the wrinkles, the pouches, the patchwork veins that seemed, almost, to belong to someone else. She closed her eyes and let the heat and steam seep and steep and coddle her.

Catching a glimpse of that sneak Manny, all of twenty-two or three, poking his head in for a look, she wagged a wet finger. "Mmm, mmmnh—not yet, you," she said out loud. But she stretched her legs and back and remembered—not him, not his face yet--how she'd preened and let him look at her lying in the tub like this when she was twenty or twenty-one. That was the first time they'd run away to a motel and the first time he'd seen her or any woman naked and not be afraid to let him see. Look at the twitch in that smile—he was ashamed! Yes, he had been, ashamed and excited.

Greeting the sabbath bride—that was how Manny's father used to talk about preparing for Friday dinner (her own parents had never bothered much with ceremony), and when Mother Bloch lit the candles on the sideboard Etta felt a thrill at the mysterious glow that extended beyond the flickering light.

Tonight, though, as she drew on a brand new pair of pantyhose and the dress she'd retrieved yesterday from the cleaners, clipped on earrings, and spooned out the casserole with its raisins and winy aroma, she nursed, playfully, a deliberate confusion—yes, she was preparing for the sabbath bride but, after all, she was the bride herself.

Making one concession to the time, she set two candles on the dinette and lit them quickly without a blessing. And standing, ate the casserole and a stalk of steamed broccoli, and sipped at a healthy dose of sweet wine poured into a juice glass.

The synagogue was walking distance up the hill towards Court Square. The night, however, had turned raw with a gusty wind. Already half a block up the street, Etta halted with a sigh, swung around, and hurried back inside the house to fetch a plastic scarf to protect her hair and a woolen one for her throat.

Near the top of the hill, only a single lamp above the doors of the synagogue lighted the front path. There hadn't been any trouble to speak of in years, but out of habit the small community of Jews in a Southern town didn't like to draw attention to itself. Perhaps that was the reason their century-old redbrick building might easily have been mistaken for a church.

Etta hung back in the shadows across the street, trying not to shiver. It was a sparse crowd tonight—half-a-dozen families, a straggler here and there. Harry and Sarah Abrams appeared, Mordecai Smith hurrying along behind them. The Levys arrived three minutes late as usual, dragging along their boy Philip who was shameless about not brushing his teeth—had already chipped two playing football—and who traveled all the way to Richmond once a week to study with the rabbi for his bar mitzvah.

At last the coast was clear, and Etta scurried across the street and up the steps. Cracking the heavy door open, she slipped inside. Tucked in one corner of the foyer, a narrow flight of wooden stairs led to the gallery, from the days when there were enough orthodox families for their women to cloister by themselves. Most of the time now the gallery was deserted, except when the choir performed from up there or when, sometimes during the high holidays, there were enough visitors from out of town or children home from school to cause an overflow from the small sanctuary. Or when on Friday evenings Etta hid herself away.

She had flowers to tend. To avoid being caught up in conversation with her friends or having to pretend to follow the service on their terms, she tiptoed up the wooden steps. Truth to tell, she'd never been much of a synagogue goer—that had been left to Manny on the rare occasion when he felt like it, on a Saturday morning or for the *yahrzeit* memorials of his parents.

Quietly she slipped onto a bench two rows back from the rail. No one directly below could see her. Only Harry or Mordecai standing way up front on the bima might be able to, but they'd have to stare hard to make her out in the shadows so high above.

Because tonight was nothing special—no particular holiday or bar mitzvah—the rabbi hadn't driven up from Richmond. And so also from long habit the congregation made do for itself. Men and women took turns reading on the bima. (The handful of more traditional Jews in town, offended by such innovations, would take their own turn in the morning).

Etta had smuggled in Manny's old prayerbook, its cover a tattered grey cipher without characters, its pages frayed. Skipping ahead of her friends below, she opened the book where a scrap of paper held her place at the *kaddish*, the prayer for the dead. Quiet, simple, reassuring, this had always been her favorite part, even before she'd lost her Manny and Jake.

Our help cometh from Him, said the prayer. *The departed whom we now remember have entered into the peace of life eternal. They still live on earth in the acts of goodness they performed and in the hearts of those who cherish their memory.*

She read the words silently and then again, whispering to make it official and buoy herself in the right mood. And shivered with pleasure. Yes, this was what she'd been waiting for, a magic incantation that released her memories and made them blossom. Here she didn't feel guilty; she was performing a solemn duty, not merely indulging herself. Keeping a finger at the spot, she closed the book in her lap, stretched her legs as far as the benches allowed, and closed her eyes.

Her memories had gathered themselves as delicately pressed flowers in between the pages of another ancient volume. Back and forth she fingertipped lightly, catching glimpses of Jake across nearly thirty years, and of Manny young and not so young. A single leaf caught her eye, and off she leapt, chasing a flash of water at a lake high in the mountains where they went swimming. Hadn't the car broken down? Yes, there was Manny in a soaked undershirt awkwardly, hopelessly prying into the guts of his pride-and-joy Buick on the dirt road. Etta put her hand to her mouth and coughed a little giggle into it. Manny tinkered and tinkered and couldn't fix a machine for the life of him.

The sight of the two-tone, turquoise and cream automobile scratched up a smell she couldn't identify right off. It was sour and unpleasant, but she couldn't let go until she recalled—That was it, the stale smoke and beer (and moonshine if his buddies could make the right connections) that soaked the front seat of the car and Jake's hair and jacket in the morning after he'd snuck home only a few hours earlier. She grimaced and waved the thought away—that wasn't the sort she wanted, not at all.

Down below in the sanctuary, Sy Rappaport was leading a responsive reading with the twenty-five or thirty worshipers. First his thin, nasal tones would drift up (Sy had moved from Brooklyn fifteen years ago, and from what his accent gave away it might have been yesterday), followed by the smudge of other voices rising and falling and indecipherable.

Manny winked at her. He was wearing his favorite suit, a natty chocolate brown, with suspenders and a red bow tie, all still new, which meant he couldn't have been more than forty. And a felt hat, darker brown, cocked to the side. Her heart winced tight. Wasn't it really back then that Manny had blossomed, right about forty? No longer the shy Jewish boy out of place anywhere beyond his own doorstep in the Southern town; not yet the sad, resigned old man who shouldn't have been old so soon. Here he was winking at her. He swung to show profile, pulling in his belly and touching his nose with a laugh—no way to pull that schnozzer in. But what did it matter? he'd demand, elbow in your ribs. You know what a big nose means in other areas.

And her heart did ache because she knew what it meant and knew why he'd blossomed back then. Natalie Coles, the wife of a buyer up in Staunton, was making him feel quite the Cavalier. For days after he'd snatched a visit with that little tramp, Manny'd be strutting around, attempting lamely to hide these proud, astonished smiles. (One horrible night they'd all had dinner together; Etta pretending not to know; poor Barney Coles, a kind, enormous radish of a man, really not knowing.)

Etta shook her head to clear away such thoughts. They were spoiling the evening—what could they possibly matter anymore?

Philip Levy, the boy with chipped teeth, was standing on the bima holding up a silver cup and croaking the blessing on the wine. His own voice dangled him helplessly, a classroom specimen of anguished puberty.

Try as she might, Etta couldn't tug loose of the sour memories. Tonight they were powerful and insistent. So vivid she could zero in on the smallest detail: the coat button sewn on by other fingers, the smell about him when he snuck home at the end of the day—that musky smell of his own after sex, laced with Natalie's catbox scent. It made her furious. "Come on, honey," Etta said, cooing and tugging him by the wrist. "Aren't you sleepy? I'm sleepy."

"It's not even six o'clock." Triumph still dilated his eyes, though they'd narrowed suddenly with alarm.

"What's that matter?" she said. She pulled and dragged and nudged him into their bedroom. Reaching under his jacket, she snapped his suspenders. But didn't let him take off his clothes. Just yanked his trousers open and hitched up her dress and slipped herself onto him standing by their bed. Oh, and he was aroused, miserable, the smells of the three of them commingling.

And in the balcony of the synagogue she too was miserable and breathing through her mouth. She rubbed knuckles hard into her eyes, over and over, trying to shake herself free. She was embarrassed with herself.

But Jake would help her out. She hadn't paid him enough attention so far tonight anyway. His eyes, the most beautiful dark eyes when he was a boy—everyone said that's what he got from her and it was true.

First thing in the morning she'd slip into his room in her robe without even turning the light on. He lay curled on his side, and she settled next to him, combing fingers through his hair, rubbing his back to wake him for school. She could feel him wake through her fingers. At last the ten-year-old turned over and looked at her, his face lighted from the doorway, his sleepy eyes dark and deeper than deep, unfilled yet with the distractions of the day. "Do I gotta?" he yawned. But once he was out of bed she could hear him whistling the latest song as he got ready.

Could those girls of his wake him with so much love? she wondered, and then bit her lip. Why was she getting into that?—That was all so much later. Jake was still in school, too young, too young for all that.

It was Manny's fault, what went wrong with Jake. He'd been undermining her all along. The two of them, man and boy, took each other's side—and where did that leave her? "Screw college, if he doesn't want to go away to college," Manny said. "Isn't there plenty for him to do here, if that's what he wants?" Just to spite her, that's why he was saying it. And she wanted to hit him, her fingers sore from twisting and tearing at each other. And Jake standing off to the side, thinking his own thoughts and apparently not even listening to them argue. What kind of example was Manny? Etta was trembling with anger, the taste of salt on her lips for the first time in a long time and she not even wiping at the tears, alone in the gallery.

A car door slammed, waking her. She'd hold her breath waiting, and yes, there, the second door slammed. So he was bringing her home again. But why assume it was the same one?—Jake was bringing another, a different one each time.

He made no effort to be quiet entering the house. The girl did, but she was drunk and giggling despite herself and though she was trying to tiptoe it wasn't possible in those heels, them striking the floor like a hammer every second or third step.

Manny hadn't stirred, but Etta knew he was awake beside her, listening. Was this an arrangement he and Jake had come to? Did Jake even bother to close his bedroom door? Because they, she, could hear it all, could hear the clothes hitting the floor, and the groping, the first great squawk of the bed, the moans, the rhythm, the cries in the night. So vivid, so vivid, to the smallest detail she was remembering.

Only dimly was she aware that the service below was ending, the small congregation wending through the aisles and out of the sanctuary. With a sudden harsh click the lights disappeared. And Etta sat in darkness. Only the faint red flicker of a hanging lamp up above the bima, the one never extinguished, remained and grew brighter, blowing shadows everywhere as her eyes adjusted. It was very quiet now.

Two car doors slammed again, nearly in unison this time, and Jake was strutting up to the house in broad daylight no less, both arms around the cute little girl at his side (Meg Tillich, wasn't it?, who'd been a couple years behind him at school and had gone off to Roanoke to become a beautician) so that the two kept stumbling over each other.

Fresh, potent as a morning after wind and rain, vivid as all the other memories, this particular scene Etta couldn't place. That suede jacket he was wearing was a clue—his father had given him that later, after he'd left the community college to start selling insurance fulltime.

Etta felt confused, disoriented. When she tried to leap ahead the memory became disjointed; she had to walk it through at its own pace. Where was she to see Jake and this Meg saunter up to her house? Was she watching through a window? Did he not care that she'd see? *Where am I?* she wondered.

The screen door slapped behind them. Jake and Meg didn't halt, didn't hesitate, but stumbled on towards the bedroom. And now Etta could smell the alcohol, the smoke, the girl's not-so-cheap perfume. How dare they? Couldn't they show the slightest decency or respect? *Where am I?*

It must have been a Saturday, because there was Manny sitting in his chair in the living room watching a Braves' game on tv. He was drinking too—beer, despite what it did to his system.

Etta found herself panting, frightened in the dark balcony of the synagogue. A thousand tiny claws clattered on the roof, driven by a hard wind. From one of her deep coat pockets she dug out a ball of kleenex and wiped her eyes, blew her nose. That last memory had unnerved her. It was so clear, so real. It frightened her not to remember when it happened. *Silly thing, silly me*, she thought. "Silly," she said softly aloud.

Yet the niggling memory tempted her back to discover where it led. The secret lay crouched waiting for her. She could keep it at bay and concentrate on the sounds and drafts and musty smells of the sanctuary. Or she could leave. She could simply walk away. Surely her responsibility to Manny and Jake extended only so far, and not to any memory like that. Sighing, she blew her nose again. Her fingers were very cold. (This would be a bad winter for her chilblains.)

The sharp hiss of the eggs startled her as they hit the hot skillet. Manny's specialty, with a liberal dash of tabasco, garlic, black pepper—and the magic touch, fresh ginger. Etta stared at her husband. His very round face was accentuated by the bald dome of his head, grey tufts around the sides. Except they weren't grey. They'd gone quite white. And he'd grown jowly, more jowly than she'd recalled.

From the way he was pursing his lips she could tell that the beer he'd been swigging in front of the tv was disagreeing with him. Gas mainly. "Shouldn't you know better?" she might have whispered aloud. But Manny was attending to the eggs. You couldn't let them grow too hard and dry in the skillet. *Why aren't I making a salad?* Etta wondered. *Why don't I remember any of this, even though I'm remembering it?*

The smell of eggs and spice drew Jake out of his room, buckling his belt and tucking in a clean shirt. That girl, that Meg, was she still in bed or had she somehow snuck out when Etta wasn't looking? Jake was whistling—he was always such a remarkable whistler, whistled any tune note for note after one hearing.

She missed him so, wanted more than all the world simply to hold him, to nestle him in her arms, all that he'd done to disappoint her no matter, absolutely beside the point.

He walked into the kitchen and put the kettle on for coffee. Said something to his old man that Etta missed, couldn't make out. Manny shrugged and replied without looking up. But again she didn't catch what he said. It wasn't that she couldn't hear their voices—she could, oh yes, just the way they'd always sounded, gruff with each other and matter-of-fact—but the sounds were muffled, the edge of the words blurred.

Confused, anguished, she wanted to cry out to them. "Oh," she moaned, knowing she couldn't speak to a memory. "Damn, damn. Damn."

Manny expertly divided the eggs with a spatula and slipped portions onto two plates. The rest he left in the skillet and covered with foil on the stove. He and Jake sat down, and there was a third place at the table with an empty plate. For her? Or for Meg still in the bedroom?

Jake rose to get the coffee, and as he was standing at his father's side, posed to pour, Etta's glance traveled up his arm and to his face and now at last she saw what she should have seen all along, the scar along the line of his jaw and up round his ear and just under his eye, healed, faint, undeniable. And she knew that if he was there like that then she had to be the one who was missing. The empty place was not for her.

The steps down from the gallery were treacherous, dark and steep. She made her way slowly, a hand pressed against the plaster. Once she'd reached the ground, however, the front door presented no problem. Three or four paces directly across the foyer it greeted her fingers, and the bolt turned easily. Of course the old men arriving in the morning would fuss at the carelessness of that casual Friday night crowd leaving the door unbolted.

The sidewalk seemed to stretch forever down from Court Square. Her feet ached and she was perspiring and she was also chilled to the bone by the time she reached her door. Only for the lock stubbornly to refuse her key. Perhaps it was the wrong key. Perhaps—and the half-second's thought terrified her—she'd come to the wrong house.

No, a thousand signs, the mat, the mezuzah on the doorpost, reassured her at once. It was only her nerves, only her hand trembling a bit. And with that the key slipped home.

Without taking off her coat, Etta went directly into the kitchen and put the kettle on for tea. She sat in the chair where Manny had been sitting—would have been sitting if the memory had ever happened, which it hadn't, except that it had seemed more real than all the others. Warm house or no, she was still trembling lightly like a bird.

A whistle began, low and tentative but swelling rapidly towards a shriek. She glanced at the kettle, an old red thing with a wooden handle, fifteen-year's-worth familiar and yet tonight threatening, foreign, not at all what she'd remembered. Didn't stop her, though--she'd be damned first. Lifted that kettle, poured water into a cup, dipped the tea bag, added milk.

Again she settled in the chair, her coat still on, cowering and refusing to look about. The tea was strong and hot and reassuring. This was all it took. Once she got to bed and to sleep and dreamed some honest dreams everything would be all right.

She realized, suddenly, that she'd left Manny's prayerbook in the gallery. It had been so dark she hadn't been able to check about or notice it lying on the bench beside her. *Too bad*, she decided with a shrug. Why did she care? What use would it be now?

She sipped her tea and felt better, stronger. It had given her a nasty turn, what she'd glimpsed. Shook her to her bones. Manny and Jake—what a pair. They deserved each other. *What a pair of bastards.* They didn't care. Not an iota. Didn't miss her at all, didn't bother to remember her. Nothing. Why should they trouble themselves?, that's what they figured. What kind of gratitude was that for all her years of faithfulness?

She sighed, rose, and poured another cup—what did it matter if it kept her up a little while longer? Her legs were aching, and it was good to sit back down.

And she nodded to a further truth that blossomed across the table through the steam and sweet tea and milk. Well, after all, what of it if they were such bastards? Hadn't she suspected it all along, down deep, that Manny and Jake were wild flowers and didn't really need her tending? Oh, they'd tolerate her remembering them, they'd let her fuss. But only because it made her feel better. Which was nice. Certainly none of it was necessary.

Sipping the last of her tea and not wishing to get up or turn out the light, Etta Bloch was feeling better, rather relieved. They must have cared something for her after all.

Hypotenuse

His Mam snatches at his hair, twisting him through the front door, and jerks him face-to-face against the sister he recognizes before she speaks and whose existence he's never suspected. Her hair's wrong. Too pale. Yes, and the flat cheekbones. But her eyes—they're what give it away—yellow cats-eye streaked like an old marble, like Mam's.

Him she hardly sees. Him she dismisses as after the fact, as irrelevant. She sluffs his presence off with a shrug as Mam says, "This'd be your brother. This here's Joshua."

The girl flicks him a look, flicks her stringy pale hair out of her eyes, scowls slightly, dismisses him once more.

"I found you," the girl says. "You didn't think I could, didn't want me to, did you? But I did."

"I told *her* I didn't want you to," Mam is saying, blaming the sack-heavy woman Josh only now realizes is standing in the corner. The woman wears a dirty raincoat and a plastic hat and she's wringing her hands.

Now she's talking to him too, now that he's noticed her, the social worker is, whingeing, yammering, a sound no one pays attention to. An angry jay. The three others, the mother and her two children, they've already settled onto three hard mismatched chairs, as if this part of the dance was choreographed before the house was bought, before Joshua was born. It's a lame triangle, mother facing daughter, daughter confronting mother, son and brother locked out, locked out and scared.

And the social worker's stoking her own indignation: how it's a betrayal of trust, how this's never happened before. "By the book, that's how I did it," the social worker swears. "Didn't I come by and see you," she says to Mam, "after she showed up first time to the agency to track you down? And you said no. Not then, not ever."

The only color in the woman's sagging face is a red-rimmed outrage. She's chanting it now, how the girl—the girl's name, the one she's taken from her other parents, is Shannalyn—how Shannalyn got into the files. Did something filthy to the janitor, she did. Enough so he'd go and let her have anything she wanted. "It's a crime, that's what it ought to be. And it's not *my* fault. I followed her out here soon as I figured what was up. If she's doing that sort of thing to find you—*well*." And the yammering ceases suddenly, jay striking home.

"You're my mother," Shannalyn says as if there's never been another sound. "I was first and I'm yours and you can't deny me no more."

Josh's Mam is smoothing the skirt across her lap. Over and over she pushes at it, kneads it, smooths it. "I had you," she admits. "That I remember all right. Just to look at you, ain't no doubt."

But Mam's face gives nothing away. She blinks at Shannalyn. Her mouth's crimped a thin grey line, same as when—Josh was there to see—her own mother finally, finally, finally gave in and let death take her too late to do her any good.

"You, Joshua," his mother sighs as if she's forgiving him though he's done nothing to deserve it. "You go on and get your sister here a drink of water. Get her one too," she says, not motioning to the woman abandoned in the corner. "They'll be on their way soon enough."

He rises, breaking the triangle, and Shannalyn looks up from under at him, cats-eyes yellow mean. Her hunger he feels in his own belly, and her hatred. In the kitchen he fetches no water. Climbs on a stool. Bit by bit, he chews at the heel of a breadloaf, stale, tough, ashen.

Rivalry

Jeremy's father would never lay a hand on him. Nor would he hit the younger children, Caryn and Luke. But to Luke this seemed beside the point—Jeremy was the oldest, his father's favorite.

In his own absolute safety Jeremy grew marrow sure and entirely unconscious. But Luke happened to be watching his brother at the moment when the truth first struck him—Jeremy—as odd, as astonishing. That he should be beyond reach. This happened on the same day when their mother murmured to him, "You should stand up for me—you shouldn't let him."

She wasn't crying any longer. She didn't sound angry or accusing, merely matter-of-fact, as if this too were a truth Jeremy had known all along, or should have known, if he were any kind of son. Luke saw his brother's shoulders stiffen with resentment as the strangeness of his situation occurred to him.

The calm, the exhaustion, the relief of a battle just past lingered in the air, an acrid smoke that was sharp and familiar. Their mother showed few visible signs of the beating she'd taken before her husband's fury flung him out of the house, blood flowing down his own cheek from a deep gash at the corner of the eye. This his wife had inflicted with a wild flail of her nails even as he'd cornered her at last, after pursuing her slowly, relentlessly from room to upstairs room of the old house. Her husband's face was red, his brow trembling, spit flying, tie flapping over his shoulder. "*Whore*," he bellowed. "*Tramp.*"

The sound of his rage filled the whole large house, even more terrible to the children cowering and watching from a bedroom than the physical blows thudding against their mother. At last their father stormed from the house, leaving her sobbing in desolate triumph. She was younger than he and darker, lonely and calm and strong.

Her eyes were puffy from weeping. Her lips were puffy too, though not from weeping. Gingerly she bathed her face with cold water while Jeremy watched from behind, studying his mother's features in the mirror above the basin. In turn, Luke and Caryn watched from the doorway of the large bathroom behind him. Caryn's hands were picking, picking at themselves as she didn't quite study her mother, her heavy reddish hair flopping every which way.

"You should stand up for me," Mama said, "you shouldn't let him."

Luke saw her words strike his brother. Mirrorward, she was staring directly into Jeremy's blue eyes, which grew dark and broody. Her own jaw was clenched. Luke sensed that she understood very well what she was doing.

Jeremy's face slowly twisted into a dark scowl. With sudden terror Luke wondered whether his brother, tall now and lean as willow, would lash at their mother himself for pointing out his shortcomings? Would he hit her? Would he cry? Luke almost shouted out to warn his mother, to stop him. But Jeremy controlled himself. Or no, that wasn't it, it wasn't control: he folded the anger and hurt and shame round and drew them into himself. They writhed in his throat and disappeared. And Luke, still watching from the safety of the bathroom door, panted with relief as Jeremy turned and pushed past him, his face stony, his eyes on something very far away.

Their mother lowered her face once more to the basin. Again and again she heaped the water against her skin, until Luke felt the hollowed-out numbness cold in his own flesh.

"Dammit—can't you stop? *Jeremy*. Don't push him any more." Their father, exasperated, pale, pleaded with the boy.

Without any direct acknowledgment, Jeremy shoved Luke roughly against the ball return. Then, pushing him aside, he heaved a full-sized bowling ball off the rack, wagged it contemptuously in his brother's face, and turned back to the lane. But the ball was too heavy for him. It skidded out of his hands, lumbering awkwardly down the lane. At least it avoided the full humiliation of the gutter. Two pins waggled and collapsed. Lips pressed thin, Jeremy turned nonchalantly and wiped his fingers on his pants.

As usual at this hour they were the only ones in Strike-'n-Spare Alley, Jeremy and his father, and Caryn and Luke. Half the lanes were cloaked in a darkness that wasn't quite cool, though it shielded them from the dust and blinding light of an August Sunday afternoon. But the warmth pawing at the hanger-like building from outside kindled a stench of spilled beer, dirty socks, mildew.

Jeremy, impatient and irritable, had seemed to be wading chest-deep through mud as he selected the bowling shoes with a large 9 on the back. He was preoccupied, seemed to be listening to a far-away sound, preparing himself. Standing behind, waiting his turn after Caryn, Luke had sensed growing danger; Jeremy's temper could ignite as quickly as their father's.

These Sunday afternoons at the bowling alley were one bead of a rosary (their mother was Catholic and the metaphor was one she'd mockingly chosen), counted off from week to week, of what a surgeon could imagine to share with his children. Monday through Saturday he'd be gone before breakfast on the long commute to his hospital in the working-class neighborhood of the city, returning after their bedtime, if he managed to make it home at all. So Sundays he salvaged for his children. Once or twice a month they'd drive to a movie. A ball game when the weather was good. In desperation they'd spend a day at home watching colorized movies or golf together.

They hated it, the three of them did. They dreaded these forced holidays with all their hearts and yet pretended to enjoy themselves for their father's sake. Did Dad know that? Luke sometimes wondered. Did he realize that their enduring the stiff, lonely hours was a mark of love? Had he come to hate the stink of the bowling alley as much as they? Or did his more general misery overwhelm such specifics?

Early that morning Luke had tugged on jeans and a shirt and slipped past Jeremy's bed to the stairs. His father, up for hours out of habit, had finished his coffee, was just clipping the leash on Parson, their springer spaniel. A year or so earlier the dog, a runt of a puppy and nearly blind, had scratched her way through the screen of the back door in late winter, hungry, wounded, desperate, while Doctor Rosen lay ill in his own hospital, nearly dead from meningitis. Caryn had (secretly at first) adopted the pup, nursed her, and together the family smuggled her one day into the hospital room as a surprise for their father's convalescence. He'd been stupefied that they could break every rule so brazenly. (But hadn't wanted to yield Parson up when time came for him to rest.)

Crouching in the shadow on the stairs, Luke hesitated until he'd read his father's mood. He was wearing pants from an old suit, too baggy for him now, hanging loose on their suspenders. His shirt sleeves were rolled to the elbow. Absently, pondering something else entirely, the doctor was bending over the dog, scratching her ears and snout. Luke noticed how sparsely the hair had grown back over his father's scalp and purple scar-seam after the surgery that had peeled him open and saved his life. His father was an old man—that's what came home to Luke with a stinging clarity—he could've, should've been his grandfather.

Jeremy sometimes told stories of a time when his father would take the stairs by two, would toss the ball once, twice before rushing off to his patients, would stay up late drinking whiskey with friends and still be fresh in the morning. But this was all legend for Luke. He couldn't remember or share. For him the sour reality had been a series of illnesses stealing his father's youth away. The murmured possibility of death sealed off anything beyond the near horizon. (*Can you teach me golf in the spring, Dad?* Jeremy had asked. *If I'm still here*, his father replied, gouging his three children with anguish.)

And his rages—wild, uncontrollable. What touched them off? Luke often wondered. *Your father sometimes is sick that way too*, their mother explained. This verdict offered both an excuse and an all-encompassing blame. She'd bite her lip, pick at it till it bled, look away.

Out of his head. That was a phrase Jeremy had tossed off to his brother and sister. Never to anyone else. Luke didn't understand. He knew that somehow his father imagined things about what his wife did while he was working. About other men, about wild fun and secret meetings. It was crazy. Was it crazy? Of course it was crazy. But Luke also sensed that his Mama kindled him: she coaxed his rage alight defiantly, a way of taunting the older man she'd married and now spent so much time nursing.

But this morning Luke, wary, spied no hint of temper. His father seemed tame, if a bit distracted. Jeremy and Caryn still lay asleep upstairs. Mama, asleep or not, remained hidden in the big bedroom. His father was stroking the dog's head, flapping the leash against his leg as if trying to remember something. Luke slipped up against him and the doctor absently patted his second son's head too.

Together they set out into the early morning light. Rising out of the creek below the house and its small stand of willows, last remnant of a larger wood, the sun seemed to gather itself, waiting to splay the full weight of summer across the countryside. Luke smelled the faint dew on the grass even as it was drawn off into the air, hovering like an echo.

His father apparently had no particular destination in mind for their stroll. No shops or pretty vistas lay in easy reach anyway. He'd bought this property, once a small farm, when it was surrounded by other poor farms and alfalfa fields. But just in the last year or so suburban developments had begun to harry it on all sides, gradually sealing the old house and five remaining acres in on themselves. From time to time the doctor, city boy himself, walked along the roadway, through the lanes and fields, as if measuring a campaign already abandoned.

Heat blossomed stealthily as they turned out along the main road. Dust and gravel spread away to the left. Freshly spilt asphalt was melting into a black goo on their right. Hardly hesitating, the doctor led them into the worn channels and along the rills of the hard-packed yellow dirt road. But it wasn't long before perspiration broke across his brow and seemed to disorient him. Halting, he gazed indecisively towards a far bend where the gravel and dirt had been washed away by snow and spring rains. Parson tugged at the leash, whining. At last Luke seized his father's hand and gently turned them, the three of them, back towards the lane from which they'd emerged.

As they limped at last down the drive to the house his mother was waiting in the doorway, worried or impatient, smiling now with relief as they approached. Luke had been leading, guiding, and as he released his father's fingers he felt a small and secret squeeze. Startled, he glanced up.

"No more," their father warned. "Listen to me, Jeremy. That's enough."

"Or what?" the boy demanded, slapping at Luke's ear and shoving him hard to the deck. Caryn, daring forward, tugged at Luke's hand to draw him clear.

"Or what?" the doctor repeated in disbelief. For an hour now, teasing his brother, plucking and pinching him, Jeremy had also been harassing his father, goading the old man, taunting him.

Luke pushed Caryn's hand away. Flushed and sweaty, he lay sprawled on the hard apron behind the alley lanes. A blaze of hatred swelled in him, rushing to his head, tingling in his limbs. His father didn't care that it was *him* who was wronged, just that Jeremy was defiant, challenging his authority. Jeremy didn't care either, didn't even notice.

Luke rose to a knee and, sprung by an anger that flushed violently through his throat and limbs, he leapt at his brother. Clawing at Jeremy, swiping at him, he yearned only to hurt him, to make him notice.

The older boy brushed aside his brother's first wild blows, hardly aware of the assault, then turning to it with a harsh laugh as Luke's kicking and swinging and lunging began to annoy him. Stepping clear, Jeremy flicked a fist and caught Luke under his right eye. It staggered the younger boy.

Tears welled up, blinding Luke. Pain flared to match his fury. It throbbed in his face and he ignored it. He welcomed the hurt as a kind of gift, a discovery of what he could endure. Again he launched himself at Jeremy. He scrabbled at him, desperate to share the gift. The anger, the pain, the rush of exhilaration lifted him so that he could hardly breathe. He was soaring.

Jeremy winced under his brother's fresh attack. Again he jabbed, harder this time. His fist smashed through Luke's arms, landed on his mouth, cut him, splayed him suddenly onto the floor. Blood dribbled through Luke's lips as he tried to rise once more.

But in that same instant a blow caught Jeremy on the shoulder, slipped and glanced off his head. Not even a blow, a gesture, a despair. Together, astonished, Jeremy and Luke and Caryn realized that their father had struck him. For a single long moment the three of them and their father remained very still, frozen in a new orientation, a new dance step suspended in the air. This was what Jeremy had been after all along—they grasped that too, his brother and sister did; maybe Jeremy only realized it at that moment as well—and he could gloat now, martyred. Their father stood above them, startled with himself, white with an anger already exhausted.

Jeremy's lips tightened into a sneer as he turned away. All of Luke's anger drained at the sight and he felt very cold. He realized for the first time that Jeremy was nearly as tall as his father if not as heavy—he could have hit back but didn't deign to.

"I told you, I begged you." The doctor spoke at last. He was shaking his head. He seemed shrunken and frail, as after the last illness, baffled by what had happened and short of breath. His eyes were puffy with sadness, as if a prophesy had borne itself relentlessly true. Beads of sweat dampened his thin, greying hair to his scalp. "I told you. Why'd you have to keep after your brother that way?"

Jeremy broke free, blue eyes aflame, face pale and stern but with a barely masked giddiness. He was already tearing off his bowling shoes and heading toward the counter. He was wounded and righteous and triumphant.

Luke remained on the ground. His father had pressed a handkerchief on him and he was wiping at the blood where his teeth had gashed his upper lip. He felt an awe at what had swept him up and washed over him, and at what had come of it. He also felt guilty, as if somehow he'd done more than participate, as if he'd choreographed the dance by insisting on his own right to be noticed.

"What's wrong?—What happened?" their mother demanded. Silence and dismay hung like a shroud over her family as they drifted into the house earlier than usual. Sullen, not answering, Jeremy pressed past her and fled to his room. Behind her, enveloping them now, were the smells of a Sunday dinner prepared while the house had been blessedly her own.

"Jeremy picked a fight with Luke. That's all." Caryn, middle child, spoke up quickly, trying to shut all else out and gather peace. Luke nodded and held up the bloody handkerchief. Together they wanted to end the matter before their father arrived.

But he was already behind them, shaking his head. "I hit him," he said, his voice shuddering with disbelief.

"Hit who?" demanded his wife.

"Jeremy. I hit Jeremy." He was already holding up his hands to ward off her words. Something had been settled for him and, helpless, he was surrendering, though perhaps to no one but himself. "No—I know. It's time. This isn't possible."

Luke saw an equal disbelief flood his mother's dark eyes, a surging horror. "You hit him?" she cried softly as if she couldn't let the fact go. "What did he do? How did he make you?"

But her husband had already turned away and was climbing the stairs, puffing with the effort. He disappeared and it seemed that they—his wife, Caryn, Luke—could not, dared not move until he came into view once more. But when several minutes later he did reappear he was carrying a valise and his medical bag. "I'll send for the rest," he said.

Caryn had settled to the carpet, dark red hair hanging over her face as her hands picked and picked. Luke watched, always watching, and wishing desperately now that some of the anger or some of the pain that had buoyed him beyond all caring in the bowling alley would return to console him. In his right hand he felt a faint pressure where his father had squeezed his fingers that morning, only that morning.

His mother hadn't moved from the front hallway. She was shaking her head as if to make sense of fragments, of nonsense. Luke had never seen her arms wag so awkwardly. Her husband walked heavily past her, but this time neither of them managed to speak. As the door closed behind him she seemed to shrink, suddenly aged too, diminished. Craning her face up the stairs she called, "Jeremy. Jeremy!" But to this command her son did not respond.

Concert

The morning's chill seemed sharper as Daniel met it again after growing warm on the tram. He hurried on, a bundle wrapped in newspaper and twine under his arm as he bowed forward into the breeze. His hip always ached when the cold was new, and he was limping slightly.

Saturday morning was still young enough that the street he turned onto was nearly deserted. Thirty yards ahead, however, two men were walking a few paces apart, their heads safely tucked down so that neither glanced at the other nor to the side nor back towards Daniel. One of them also carried a small package. They all made for a dark iron fence behind which a green cupola rose above a line of young trees.

Inside, in the lobby, a few men gathered in tight fists of conversation. Daniel waved to one, acknowledged another with a smile, but slipped past to avoid being caught up in their talk. A younger man than the rest, disheveled and slouching aggressively against a door, caught his eye and nodded with a sour grin. Daniel didn't smile. He nodded too and moved on deliberately through the entrance. He didn't know this Mikhail well, and he neither liked nor trusted him.

The package still under his arm, he came forward into the shadows of the sanctuary, tugging a small cap from his pocket. The service was already underway, most of the usual congregation in their places. The cantor's voice carried across the deep rows of wooden benches. Daniel drifted quietly towards his seat, bequeathed by custom, at the end of one row. Only there did he unbutton his coat and carefully draw the American prayer book from its sheath of newsprint. He stowed the paper and twine under the bench. With English on every second page the book wasn't really a *siddur*; they'd even pared away some of the Hebrew. But enough was there, or if not quite enough it didn't bother him because he could wander slowly off with the English, letting it roll silently on his tongue.

They were standing for prayer, the men of the congregation, when a whispered wave of attention swept past Daniel. He glanced back over his shoulder and saw, as he expected, that a foreigner had come into their sanctuary. This one was alone, a tall man and rather heavy, and he strayed along to perch in an empty row. He'd sense enough, at least, to wear a hat.

German, perhaps American, Daniel guessed from habit. This game he was good at, catching hints in their clothes or faces and making a guess. He'd played it for years with the foreigners and with music on the radio (guessing the composer), when his radio worked. Oh yes, he could spot the real thing. This one's suit was all right, and his shirt was colored, blue perhaps, which was better still. The informers, they slipped up on that sort of thing—shirts, more often belts—somehow they always got the belt wrong.

Some of Daniel's friends loved these occasional visits. They could pass a little gossip—the most general, the least dangerous— back and forth between worlds. The contact delighted them, but he for one was tired of it. To him they insisted on bringing the

English and Americans who weren't educated well enough to speak Hebrew or Russian or German or even a little Yiddish. Yes, he was thoroughly tired of it.

Only a month before, an American and his wife had cornered him as he came out of the sanctuary. They were prodded on by a trio of local Jews, acquaintances but not friends of his.

"You speak only English?" Daniel had asked with a smile.

"A little French too," the woman said quickly, earning a dark look from her husband.

"Yes?" He smiled more broadly. "That is good. Now, please, understand me. We have nothing for you here. It is too late except for these old men behind you. Take your look at our synagogue—that is good, I am happy—but expect no more. Good day." The smile never left his lips as he folded his little cap and tucked it in his pocket. A few days later he'd learned how angry the other three were, muttering about his bad manners and his American book and how he shaved on the sabbath.

This morning's visitor sat quietly and looked about him. The sanctuary was a large one from the old days, and Daniel suspected that the seventy men or more would seem very few. And the handsomeness of the dark weathered benches, the grace of the dome arching overhead and of the pillars supporting the balconies, all seemed to fade and withdraw, scouring the great hall of its beauty as this one perched in the mild din of prayers and small conversations, distantly gauging these Jews. Daniel shifted in his seat to tug at a handkerchief. He snorted into it angrily. More than ever he wanted to be left alone, to let this all finish undisturbed if it couldn't finish in peace.

When, at the proper moment, three Torah scrolls were carried down and through the aisles, the stranger at last left his seat. He trailed along behind one of the scrolls to a wooden stand in a corner where eight or ten other men circled around. They signaled for him to join, now that he'd taken the first step. But he smiled, shook his head, and lingered beyond their reach. He'd be near enough, Daniel imagined from across the way, to hear the reading and perhaps catch glimpses of parchment through the thin press of bodies.

They tried again when the day's verses had been read and the Torah scroll dressed in its faded velvet. Four men gathered about the stranger in a wary knot. Daniel couldn't tell whether he was smiling or not, but he soon shrugged apologetically. So this one too spoke only English.

The other old Jews had no intention of begging Daniel again for his help, and clearly they were put off by the foreigner's coolness. The four of them nodded and bobbed sympathetically, woodenly, so as not to seem ungracious, drifting away, the last patting him on the shoulder.

Daniel was waiting. He was waiting for the service to end and their visitor to drift way, no moth from no candle. He wouldn't go to him; no, this he'd sworn to himself. They could have nothing to say, nothing to share, and soon it would be over.

But why did he stand there, hands in his pockets, not forlorn so much as pensive? Whether his thoughts had any connection with the Hebrew chant or the sanctuary or with something in another world than Leningrad, his face betrayed nothing.

Instead of returning to his first seat, the man slipped across the central aisle and along one of the empty rows to another spot in shadow near the far wall. Only a few yards away now, Daniel saw him blow on his hands. It was chilly. The boiler had abandoned them once again and with winter still to come.

Weary rather than excited, resigned to the old impulse rather than embracing it, Daniel rose and shuffled softly up to his shoulder. "You are welcome to share my prayer book," he said gruffly in English, as if a rebuff were what he wanted more than expected.

The visitor started, half-rising as he turned with a look of surprise or perhaps annoyance. Taller (and heavier) than he'd seemed at a distance, he towered over Daniel. "Sure," he said doubtfully. They stood there awkwardly for a long moment. "Have a seat," he offered.

Daniel sensed his suspicion, and almost turned back to his own bench. That *he*, the visitor, should be suspicious! And then Daniel smiled to himself—at least this one wasn't such a fool as the rest.

"How do you come to have an English book this way?" the stranger asked, pointing at it.

"A gift from a friend who visited us here—American, like you, I think."

"Actually," he said without any whisper of a smile, "I'm Canadian."

Daniel glanced at him again with renewed interest, at his clothes, the cut of his hair, and the interest slowly became doubt.

The other stared back. "*Canadian*," he said again.

Daniel shrugged. The visitor was making no effort to follow either the Hebrew or English in the book. "So, you are Canadian," Daniel said. "Are you a Jew as well?"

"That's right."

Daniel nodded, his turn to be wary.

"I'm afraid your friends over there weren't much impressed," said the stranger. "I've never been much good with languages."

"Never mind this," Daniel said. "For me it is a long time, many years, since I studied your English at university."

"Really? You'd never know it."

After such a lame start, neither of them knew how to go on, and they paid an empty sort of attention as the service neared its conclusion. Others around them were already pulling on coats, carrying their gossip and business from the sanctuary out into the lobby and street. Daniel knew they'd be watching him, wondering why he'd chosen to meet such a one as this. But he was more concerned with what was to come next; not having been to market for five days, he couldn't ask him home for lunch. The soup and bread he'd planned for himself would never stretch for two.

The visitor was fastening his coat (it was a good coat, very handsome, but a good coat), and Daniel knew that another moment would be too late. "If you wish," he said while fitting his book back into its wrappings, "we can go to my flat and make Kiddish together."

The Canadian shoved his hands into his pockets. "I'd like to," he said, "but we're here only until tomorrow. And Monday we've got a concert in Moscow. This afternoon is our only chance to tour your city, and I'm afraid they've got it all booked up."

Daniel tossed a hand as if it were no concern to him. "It is not my business to keep you."

"I don't mean any offense, all right? It's just planned and everything." He hesitated. "Look, I suppose there's no reason I can't make time to have wine with you."

Daniel glanced up at him, feeling old and annoyed, and terribly thirsty all of a sudden. "This is very kind of you," he said without warmth.

Together they queued along to the back of the sanctuary. Daniel's hip ached dully again after sitting still for so long. Mikhail, the younger man with greasy hair and more than a day's stubble, had kept his post like a faithful dog, always about to enter the hall and never quite succeeding. This time he neither smiled nor nodded to Daniel.

The late morning hadn't yielded its autumn chill. Shadows cut swathes around the synagogue while the sun was kindling the breeze good and sharp as they emerged onto Lermontovsky Prospekt. The wind whipped ahead on the pavement, catching leaves, tossing and sweeping them along. It swirled up under the skirts of Daniel's coat. With a sigh he hid from the man at his side, he conceded to the universe that he should have worn his hat.

At this hour the tram was crowded, but they managed to squeeze into two seats at the rear. They sat stiff and silent, waiting to move on. With a jarring hiccup forward, the tram began cutting its way through the city. They swayed with it. At least it was warm. The other passengers were taken with the silence as well; no one violated the easy Saturday lull.

As they swung heavily onto Nevsky Prospekt, Daniel pitched to one side into a stolid woman at least his own age. She broke his fall with her great and shapeless chest, not reeling herself and hardly noticing him, though she righted him smartly enough with her arm. He winced and thanked her, bobbing his head and cradling his package against his chest. He glanced up and discovered the Canadian smiling—but not at him. Nevsky shone on such a day. The sky was bright and clear, free of the haze and humidity of only a month before and of the full weight of cold yet to arrive.

They crossed one canal and then the narrow span of a river that fed the Neva. Water flashed, the visitor's head snapped back to the gleam already spent, and Daniel buoyed with a surge of pride. The countless colors along the city's central avenue were cool and bright as the day, fresh with autumn, flashing to match canals and golden church domes. Both men rolled with the sweep of the tram, and the light swelled with Daniel's breath, just as it had contracted into a dark knot in the sanctuary.

Only at the last moment did he realize they'd arrived at his stop. He tugged sharply at the other's sleeve. They drove out against the press of new bodies boarding the tram, Daniel clutching his package in the crook of his arm and prying through the crowd. His guest followed in the narrow wake as the doors clattered shut behind them.

Once away from Nevsky, the colors grew muted, but the canal they were strolling along remained sharp and blue and brilliant. At a distance even Daniel's apartment building seemed gay, what with the resolute pink of its four squat stories. Its inner courtyard, however, was damp and grey. Reluctantly, a little angry at his guest for forcing him to veer away from the canal and into such a grim place, Daniel pressed on, shaking his head as if it were all against his better judgment.

A brace of huge garbage containers hid the stairwell to his apartment in one corner of the courtyard. The stone steps were narrow and treacherously worn and they radiated a badly lighted chill. Daniel climbed on without stopping as he usually did at the second landing. By the third stage he was breathing heavily and, despite his efforts to hide it, his limp grew worse and his hip more painful. Every few steps the stranger grunted.

At his door Daniel fumbled for the key deep in an inner pocket. He tugged to free it and he felt a little dizzy and embarrassed and his heart was racing again the way it did which only made it harder to catch his breath. At last he urged the key into its lock and, pushing open the door, he foraged on through a cluttered entrance and into the flat's main room.

"Of course I will take your coat?" he said, still panting.

"Don't bother, for heavens sake." His visitor quickly draped the coat across the arm of a small once-yellow sofa. The window behind it, overlooking a narrow sunless alley, was already battened against the cold.

"Please, look about as you wish," said Daniel. "I will put my things away and bring the wine."

Obediently, the Canadian poked at a pile of books and journals strewn across the top of an ancient upright piano.

"My English books, the ones that are left, they are across from you, there, in the shelves," Daniel said. The other flashed a quick, uncomfortable grin, but didn't stray from the same vague area. Once or twice he glanced at the window as if expecting to find some new scene, and at his watch which did indeed change, if only slowly.

Daniel was hunting for the wine, back and forth across the room, searching the several large cupboards with bric-a-brac and pictures and still more books. Then, suddenly, he remembered. Rising sheepishly from one knee, he dragged the sofa a few inches out from the window and surfaced bottle in hand. Three inches or so of dark wine remained. Avoiding a glance at his guest, who might be smiling, he set the bottle soundly in the middle of a table, sweeping aside books and a lone porcelain geisha. He rushed to the kitchen, snatched two glasses out of the bathtub, half a loaf of bread from a shelf.

"There's no reason to go to all this trouble," the other man called too loudly from inside.

Daniel returned and set the glasses and bread next to the wine. "For these few minutes you are my guest. How can there be any trouble?" He frowned at the petulance in his own voice. "Here, come, we will say Kiddish together." He divided the wine and raised one of the glasses, as much a salute as a gesture for the man to accept it. "Can you tell me your name?"

"Joseph," he said. He shifted from one foot to the other and back again, staring down into Daniel's uplifted face. "This is your home after all. Shouldn't you be making the blessing?"

Your manners in the new world are not so very good as your clothes, thought Daniel. But he raised his glass and gave the Hebrew in a dry voice, choosing not to chant.

"Amen," said Daniel.

"Amen," said Joseph.

Without saluting each other they drained the small dose of sweet wine.

Taking his seat at the head of the table, Daniel tore two pieces from the loaf. Joseph lifted a couple of books from the other straightback chair and tossed them gently onto another pile.

The bread was very dry. Before he'd quite swallowed the piece he was chewing, Daniel looked up. "Maybe you would like vodka with this? It is all I have. Why not?"

"Not after the wine, thanks. But I wouldn't say no to some water."

Daniel nodded. He didn't know where the vodka was anyway, and if he drank now he'd have a sour stomach the rest of the day. He should have offered water in the first place. Having rinsed and filled their glasses at the tap, he returned.

The silence which had all along been heavy, grew painfully awkward. Twice Joseph secretively flipped up the wrist with his watch as he tugged at the clump of bread. Finally he took a deep breath. "So what is there you want me to do? For your friends at the synagogue. More books and letters, I suppose? That sort of thing?"

"Nothing," Daniel answered sharply with a note of triumph. His hands lay open on the table and he was staring at them. And on hearing himself he realized he'd been waiting for this, anticipating it all along. "There is nothing," he said. "At our synagogue, yes, some of them wish for such things. But you must go back there for that. Me, I want nothing. The friends I have, the other old men," he said, spreading his hands in long-extinguished fury, "we want nothing but peace and a little quiet. It is too late for all the rest."

Joseph shrugged and glanced at the window. The last thing he'd expected was to offend the old man.

And Daniel realized that at once, and knew as well that the offer had been just so much politeness. Or perhaps he didn't know until he read the embarrassment on the other's face. In this moment Daniel wanted to hate the visitor, but he felt only an ashen distaste for the scene he himself had bred.

"I am too hard on you—this is not what you mean." He sucked in at the anger and his voice was softer as he reached across and patted Joseph on the sleeve, playing now an older man to a younger. "If you like, if it is not too much trouble, perhaps you will send me some music. A recording perhaps?"

"That I can do," Joseph said, relieved, though with a hint of suspicion still in his eyes.

Daniel noticed and chose not to see. "Some Brahms?" His voice grew dark and conspiratorial as he confessed. "One of the trios perhaps?"

Joseph grinned and leaned an elbow on the table for his own confession. "I'm a cellist myself, you know. It's our orchestra here on tour."

"This is true? How wonderful!" The older man leapt up with a little grunt and opened one of the cupboards. Few of his records had sleeves. He drew one out carefully and set it on the gramophone perched on a low neat stack of books. Hunting through a drawer in the same cupboard, he found a volume of scores and rushed with it back to the table. A thin ribbon of music survived the old recording's crackle.

The paper of the score was a mottled yellow, brittle as autumn leaves. Some pages were ragged, others torn, and the necessary care it took to flip each page meant that several measures were abandoned each time.

Horn and cello stroked each other's flank as the piano wove in and out and bound the three together. Daniel needed to follow the notes of the score no more than he had the prayerbook's Hebrew that morning and he closed his eyes. Music pressed up to his throat; his pulse beat firmly against its fingers.

Abruptly, the needle popped and skipped, catching up the music in a single stuttered phrase before spinning it on. Pained, Daniel opened his eyes and met the visitor's. Neither smiled. The music raced on at an unnatural tempo, the old record whirling too quickly on the newer machine, though still resolutely harnessed to those fading black bars in the score.

As if the wine had flowed straight through to mock him, Daniel's bladder suddenly needed to be emptied. He shifted in the chair and refused to be paraded back and forth. He clenched his jaw.

The Canadian didn't check his watch again until the music ended. And even then he paused, sharing a coda of silence with his host. They didn't smile.

"I'll send on a record or two," Joseph said.

"Russians, you see, cannot play Brahms," Daniel said.

"Aren't you Russian?"

"What does it matter? If I am Russian or I am a Jew, it does not matter. The Russians still cannot play Brahms." Vertigo swept up, buoying him again with a giddy lightness. He was hungry and light-headed, his stomach growled, and he clasped desperately at the euphoria. "Again," he cried, "the last movement. We will hear it once again." As he rose from the table he saw Joseph check his watch.

The flawed tinny sound was more obvious this time, and they left the score to itself. Daniel twisted on his chair, his bladder aching. And he knew, with an ache too of dismay, that they'd lost their moment. This was too much. The music stretched on as they waited and prayed, not together, for it to end.

Daniel rose once more to his feet. "I will be back," he said and, hurrying from the room, he slipped into the cool darkness of the water closet. With a groan he fumbled with himself, sighing then with the urgent relief. He stood there, his loins straining forward, he listening and breathing deeply, holding the breath and releasing it ever so slowly at last. It wasn't so bad anymore, the rest of it. He didn't mind going back out.

The room was quiet when he returned, with Joseph standing by the yellow sofa. His coat hung open.

"I really am late to meet my people," he said.

Daniel decided that, after all, he didn't much like this man. But he wished he had just such a blue shirt.

Joseph smiled lamely. "If you'll tell me where, I'll send on your Brahms."

A small red splotch of wine had dried on the wooden table, and Daniel studied it, hesitating, before going to the cabinet where he found paper and the hard nub of a pencil. At the table he kept his back to Joseph. His name. He considered making one up. To give him his name, to write it down, that would surely be foolish. *Fool*, he thought. Carefully he printed block capitals, first Russian, then below in English. He wouldn't make up a name, not for him; he'd give his name to this one.

Joseph came and stood at his shoulder, all of his impatience concentrated in the coat hanging open by Daniel's ear.

The address, quickly. In English alone Daniel printed the number and street of the apartment he and his wife had lost during the war. *Send it to me there*, he thought, *perhaps it will find me.*

He held out the slip of paper to Joseph and together they walked to the door. Daniel felt his heart racing again. With a last smile, guilty and endlessly relieved, Joseph padded quickly down the stone steps. Daniel didn't linger, but shut and locked the door.

The vodka wasn't hidden by the sofa. It sat in the cabinet where the wine should have been. He opened the bottle and put it to his lips for a short sip, regretting it the instant it hit and twisted in his stomach. The two glasses of water were still on the table and he drained one with three long swallows.

Fool, he thought again angrily. He swallowed the loneliness and annoyance. His breath caught and he coughed, gagging, poised in the middle of the room. His eyes teared as he coughed, and he pulled the small cap out of his pocket and wiped them with it.

As his eyes stung he thought of Joseph and discovered, not without surprise, that he forgave him. He shook his head and the tightness in his chest faded as he mocked himself for forgiving anyone. "That is very good of you," he murmured.

Weary, calm, not so angry anymore, he coughed one last time to clear his throat, paused long enough to shrug and forgive himself too, and went into the bathroom to heat soup for lunch. He was very hungry. *Perhaps it will find me*, he thought, remembering the Brahms.

Advert for Love

My Minda returned home from her first day at Shri Krishna College and discovered that Subji-Auntie had spent the day with the newspapers, with *The Times of India*, *The Hindustan Times*, even *The Delhi Times*, scouring matrimonial ads. She had snipped them, Subji-Auntie did, the ones she found most promising, and arranged them in a delicate jigsaw on the dining table for Minda's parents to review.

The puzzle puzzled my Minda as she entered from the street, flushed with the excitement of her initiation into college life, and went to the kitchen for a glass of water. The little scraps of newsprint made a pattern on the table. She bent over and discovered what they contained and understood at once. She was surprised only that there were so many eligible ones—not ideal, not really possible, many of them, but *eligible*.

By that evening the puzzle had disappeared, but Minda's mother looked at her over the dinner table, worried and silent. Subji-Auntie did not look at Minda at all during the meal, but she ate a great deal and purred at her fingers, licking them clean like a satisfied cat.

Every day for two years Minda returned home to discover a fresh puzzle spread accusingly across the table. "Some very nice boys are looking for young brides," Subji-Auntie says, not every day and not to Minda, but to Minda's mother. "*Young* brides."

"I am a writer," I say to Minda, "and you are a historian. Together we can make the solution." I have a plan. My older brother Alok suggested it. Even so, it is a brilliant plan.

Minda and I met at a poetry reading of the south branch of the university—students from different colleges together. What matters is not that we talked and we had coffee, that we walked together and met, when we could, when we dared, every week for more than a year. It does not matter that we fell in love, or it matters only to us. What matters is that her family are Brahmin, Maithili Brahmin, not terribly wealthy or ambitious, but Brahmin nonetheless and they will marry her only to an auspicious candidate.

I am that candidate. My family is also from Mithila. We are Brahmin as well. My family has known her family for generations; our family name, Misra, is the same name; we are even related, cousins, but not for seven generations and that is all that matters. It is not chance that Minda and I met at the poetry reading; it is chance that we did not know each other all our lives. *I* am the auspicious candidate. Even so, we must make it seem not a love match, but a match arranged in the stars. And so it is—our parents would have made the match if it had occurred to them. But, but. If we approach through a matchmaker now it will be impossible. There is another way. Subji-Auntie's way.

> Alliance invited for educated young man with great prospects as writer. Age 21, 5'7", 60 kg. Looking for educated girl with creative abilities, modern views. No dowry. Must be Maithil Brahmin. Write Box 4777.

Minda shakes her head, bites her lip. She is already ahead of me, knows at once what I am suggesting. No pleasure allowed me: no surprise, delight, admiration for my craft. "'Educated girl,'" she says. "That's all? My family will be offended—it must be more. Beautiful. Definitely must include *beautiful*."

"Sure," I say. "Naturally."

"And you don't seem much of a catch. 'Great prospects.' Hmph—what are they? They mean nothing. What about the salary you must have? And you don't want to tell them you're a writer—that'll kill it right off, Misra or no Misra." She gives a quick, dismissive shake of her head.

"Great—see what a team we are? You're just helping me be more creative. Easy."

But she isn't through yet. "And you've got to be bigger to impress them. "Make it five-eleven and seventy kilos."

"Let's make him a real dream boat, why not?"

She snaps me a quick look, blushes.

> Alliance invited for educated, affluent young man with career. Age 24, 5'11", 70 kg. Looking for beautiful, educated talented girl. No dowry. Must be Maithil Brahmin. Contact Box 4777.

Even so, it doesn't happen right away. Hawk-like Subji-Auntie, Subji-Auntie who doesn't miss anything, she misses the ad. Three days in a row Minda comes home and studies the puzzle-of-the-day and it isn't there. Her third year of college, and to make Mummy and Daddy happy, to keep Subji-Auntie at bay, she pretends closer attention. She considers the puzzle as if everything is now possible. They are waiting, her family. I am waiting too. The stars must come together.

What I have not anticipated is that other letters will arrive. The box I gave—here was I thinking?—this Alok's idea too, it is my parents' post box. Every day now, beginning with one, then two or three, each day more, the letters arrive. Mama is puzzled. "Alok—what is this about?" she asks my brother.

He shrugs. "Must be wrong box, wrong advert, Mama. You don't find me putting ad in paper."

But Babu, he has been searching and now he finds it in the paper. "Look at this ad. If it isn't you, it seems to be you. Right size, right box, right caste even. Alok, what are you not telling us?"

Again my smooth brother shrugs innocently. "Maybe you placed ad for me, Babuji? Trying to trap me at last, are you?" He laughs.

So many Maithili girls. I had no idea. Even so many Misras, cousins beyond cousins I never heard of. They must think I'm the Maharaja of Darbhanga, they're so many, they're so eager.

On the seventh day Subji-Auntie breaks down and presents the ad, one among an extra-plentiful puzzle. Minda studies, oh no, not giving anything away. She doesn't hurry. Maybe, she thinks, she will not even notice today. The ad if we are patient will surely show up again. It will throw Auntie off the scent of scandal. But no, Minda finally taps her finger on the grey little scrap. "Hmm," she says, tapping. "This one is interesting. What do you think, Mummy?"

One father writes to the other. A photo of my Minda is included. Yes, she is beautiful. She had no need to remind *me*.

Her ears are not quite in alignment, it is true, and her chin is sharp in this photo. But Babu studies it seriously, one among several, and asks Alok what he thinks.

"Bit of a dog, seems to me," he says with a bite of toast. He is heading out the door to his new scooter dealership. "But we're being so choosy already, we cannot be moreso."

I hate my brother.

I have spent my life invisible, my brother's shadow. No, too small even to be his shadow—it would fit him only at mid-day. Cricket he played and soccer. So fast, such a star, so stupid—in school he did nothing. No, not true—he smoked, he smuggled bottles of beer with his friends.

School I could make my own. The life of the mind! The life of a writer—someday!

Babu arranges the meeting for Thursday. Minda will come with her father for inspection. My mother spends the day cooking and cleaning, harassing our servant. She will work herself up, exhaust herself, annoy herself at universal imperfection, all the better to be severe and critical of the girl. "Vijay, you come too," she says.

Astonished, I manage not to snort through my nose. Then I do not want to laugh at all.

I grab Alok when he comes home for lunch, greasy with smugness at selling his scooters. "For *you* they are matchmaking. You don't want a wife, Brother. You always say so. Tell them the match is for me," I demand angrily. "Tell them it was your idea. My Minda is coming."

"But this *isn't* you, Vijay Brother. Read the ad you wrote. Twenty-four it says. Five-foot-eleven, yes? Who is this if not me? It is your ad, you wrote it, but this is me you describe. Her father will be furious to find deceit. He will cancel everything. No, we must carry through a little farther."

Minda arrives with her father. She is all shyness and blushes. I signal her but she does not see.

A match made by the stars they all agree. Mama is put out only that she cannot find more fault. Alok is casual, condescending. He sits on a cushion and smokes, gazing in appraisal at Minda through haze and half-closed eyes. Minda squirms self-consciously and says nothing.

I am invisible again. I tear at my hair. I stomp along the walls of the room and no one sees. "This is impossible," I say aloud—I think I say aloud—but no one hears.

Outside her classroom at Shri Krishna I catch Minda by the arm. Other students look on in alarm as she snatches herself free. "Stop it," she cries.

"But Minda—this is crazy. All of it. Crazy."

"What can I do?" she pleads with a stubborn shake of her head. "There is nothing for me to do. It is arranged. Settled. For after my graduation."

"But this is all craziness," I cry. "This was to be for us, for you and me."

She shrugs. Nothing to be done, she says without saying.

"Did *he* do this? Was this arranged all along with his idea? And you? You and Alok?"

She is looking over my shoulder. "It was all in the stars," she says firmly and turns away.

BAITING

She made me uncomfortable right from the start, Miss Lucy Grimes did, when she marches in looking for a job. Jenny's the only girl working the counter—one of my black girls—and, before anything is said, no one has to tell me they know each other. They're standing there, Miss Grimes and Jenny, facing each other on best behavior.

"Nice to see you, Lucy—what can I get you?" says Jenny, her voice so sweet.

"I'd like an application, if you'd be so kind," Lucy Grimes says. "For the job you've got up in the window."

Now that rattles Jenny. "Here?" she says. I can't see her face, but I know that look of surprise, her dark eyes spread wide.

I'm standing not three feet away, and it doesn't take much brilliance to figure I'm the manager, the one to talk to, since my shirt says "manager" on the pocket. But this girl doesn't glance my way once, though she must have seen me. I understand it sure—I look different enough to throw people—but it really gets me, when they pretend not to see. Anyway, Jenny turns and checks with me. I shrug. She swings by to fetch an application from my desk. No brushing past, let me tell you, a foot clear if an inch.

Miss Grimes is busy searching for a pen in her white handbag, still not looking at me. I figure she's about Jenny's age—thirty-five—but there's no good reason for guessing that, because she's one of those black women who are somehow both younger and older than they ought to be. She's prissy neat, her hair parted in the middle and pulled back like a child's in two pigtails. Her dress is a blue jumper sort of thing with a white blouse underneath. And she's wearing *stockings*—applying for a job in a burger joint.

Get this—this is what it's all going to be like—before she'll fill out the application Lucy asks Jenny for a wet rag and wipes out a booth that's already as clean as anything's going to get. Doesn't want to soil her dress or the application form. When she's filled out every line, every blank space, back she comes to the counter, not to Jenny, but right on up to the manager. This time she's looking at me, all right, square in the face, as sure of herself as can be. Smug. Doesn't look at it—my back—no, straight at me since I'm hardly any taller than her. I don't know what's worse—when they don't look at me at all as if I'm not allowed to exist, or when they'll look me in the eye and no where else.

"I'd like a job," she says straight out. Pushes the sheet at me across the counter. Smears it after all.

"You ever work in a place like this before?" I say.

"You can see there on the form I haven't. But I've thought it would be a good thing to do." She smiles, her hands crossed in front of her, trying to look humble. Gotta be the church—how she and Jenny know each other. Because these black baptists do that—don't want you to know how proud they really are—and Jenny's got something of that in her. A little ways up the counter Jenny's busy with an order, and people are coming in behind, and you bet she's listening to Lucy and me. Her head's cocked. That's the tip-off—I can tell what *she* thinks and I should've trusted her right then and not hired Lucille Grimes. But trusting her, knowing Jenny's right when I'm supposed to be the manager—

and everyone else knowing it too—sometimes it sticks in my throat. I'll go ahead and needle her with it, that I'm the manager, forget the right and wrong of it.

I'm not looking at Miss Grimes or her application. She gets impatient. "You can check the references," she says. "I really want this job."

"What do I care about references if you haven't been in jail?" I say to shake her up. But she takes it straight, right over her head. "Be here at five-thirty tomorrow morning and we'll get you a uniform. And wear some real shoes you can walk in."

Not a word from her. She stares right at me, smiling but with her lips pursed. Oh she's pleased with herself now all right. And out of the restaurant she clip-clops in navy blue pumps.

✱

The first time Jenny and I snuck away to her place on a slow afternoon we did it real quick like it was something we had to get over. I lay there afterwards, back to her, feeling pretty funny. It was the first time I did it with a black girl. It was the first time I'd ever done it and not had to pay. It felt pretty funny. So I was lying there trying to figure it out and half asleep in the afternoon heat, and Jenny started to get to know me, starting with my ears and working from there. But she didn't finish where you'd guess—hardly bothered there. It felt so good—and I was so distracted wondering if this was all wrong—that she was already stroking and tracing circles on the hump high up my back when I snapped awake to it. It was like she was calling attention to it or mocking—that's what I'm used to anyway and I didn't know her yet. All in a single breathless pause she knew I'd realized; her hand stopped but didn't draw away; I turned on an elbow (hurts to twist like that but I didn't think); slapped her once sharp, quick, clean across the face.

Her eyes were wet at the sting, damn angry tears. She panted short and quick as we faced each other, heads up a few inches from the bed. Maybe because my head was to her now I smelled her sweat and she smelled good.

"My old man hit me before," Jenny said. "No more of that for me—you hit me again I slice your balls off."

Never with one of the white girls from work. It's all they can do to look at me and pretend there's nothing different. And it'd be bad for business if anyone found out.

My other blacks know about Jenny and me of course. Jenny's shift leaves after lunch and then I'll be gone for a couple hours. They don't like it—but then they need the job. And Jenny's a big girl. I think the others might be on me about it, job or no, but none of them wants to cross Jenny. She's sweet as can be and she can take care of herself. You don't want to get her mad.

"Jesus Christ," I say, gulping breath back. My heart's pounding me all bruises inside.

"Don't you go swearing now," she breathes into my ear while still nibbling at it, lying on me all heat and spice. I know she means it and I know she's grinning too. No way I can go back to work without a shower today—she sweating and me sweating hard and nearly dead and never so good. But who wants to move, ever?

"This one'll have to last you," she says.

"Huh?" I say.

"You went and hired Lucy Grimes and I know her real well—known her all my life. She ain't gonna be fooled and she sure won't keep quiet about it. I can just hear Reverend Jordan asking me to come on over for a little chat—no way I want that."

It's hot and dark with drawn blinds in Jenny's bedroom. I'm lying there a little scared, and angry too because she's trying to blackmail me. Pretty tough blackmail too. "I can fire her quick as I hired her."

"Don't you *do* that," she snaps quick fire. (I'm sure stumped now—don't know what the hell she's after.) "You've done it, now let her work if she wants to."

I've rolled over—grab her head, hair, arms, tuck her into me good. "What's she *want* to for?"

"Not for money, you can bet. Her daddy owns the biggest funeral home in town. I guess him or her mamma or Reverend Jordan think it'll be good for her to try a job. Good for her humbleness or something."

"Has it been good for your humbleness?"

Jenny giggles, bites my shoulder hard."I don't got to be humble that way," she says. Rolls clear of me and onto her back. "Bet she's a good worker for you."

✳

Oh she's a good worker all right. At a quarter after five next morning Lucy Grimes is waiting for me, a box tucked under her arm. When we've found her a uniform she changes in the bathroom and comes out wearing a pair of those nurses' white shoes. Soles broad as my hand. I can't help but think how by noon everyday the ache in my feet and calves draws itself high and nests up in my back. It'd look silly as hell—I'm not that hot a looker anyway, God knows—and I wouldn't mind a pair of those shoes.

Jenny's working the counter, but I send our new employee down to Louise at the other end to learn the paces. No better time than breakfast. A steady flow of customers, mostly too sleepy to cause trouble. It's about all Lucy Grimes can handle at first, helping Louise get coffee and biscuits and eggs onto our little plastic trays. Lunch, when business really starts, should be something to see.

I said before, early on, that Lucy Grimes made me uncomfortable from the start, as if I knew right then nothing good would come of all this. I should get a license and bottle my own wisdom. Because things are changing even before we get to lunch. It's in the air. Maybe all my blacks go to the same lousy church—they're Miss Lucy-ing and Miss Grimes-ing her as if she owns the place and just stopped by to check up on them. Polite and hang-dog, all of them.

Two years Louise has been with me, been through it all, and I've seen her cuss a customer right out the door for trying to pull a fast one. Well, Lucy Grimes has a tray loaded with coffee and hot apple pie and Louise goes to slide it across the counter and over it goes, all of it, everywhere on the floor, not a little on this truck driver. He's none too happy. "*Shit*," says Louise and slams a hand on the counter and starts waving her arms like she doesn't know what to do, and then on top of it all she's crying.

Well you bet I'm surprised—everyone is. Before I can do anything, Lucy Grimes has one of the boys out front wiping off the driver and mopping the floor and she's got the order all done again and ready to go. Truck driver's grumbling but content. Louise has collapsed on a stool in back. So far I've managed not to look but now I can't help but look and there's Jenny down at her end just looking at me. Christ-Almighty.

I guess I understand the white girls even worse than the blacks, because they're all taken with Miss Grimes too—think she's darling or something. They show her how to make a milkshake. Will they let her do it on her own? —Hell no—When she's there at the counter taking the orders, they're racing around behind fetching the shakes and fries and burgers.

I don't know how, but we make it through the lunch madhouse. Maybe we're simply too busy to notice disaster full in the face. Baptism (of a baptist?) by grease and sweat instead of fire, but I got to admit Lucy Grimes has held up. Except for the eternal afternoon stragglers, the counter has cleared by two o'clock. She's tapping her fingers nervously against a cash register and looking pretty good—lighter-skinned than Jenny, and there's a flush in her face, tired and hot and excited. Pretty satisfied with herself too. The white cap's slipped; neat bun of hair on her neck has come loose, though she pats at it.

One of the boys drifts out from back, mop in hand. "Miss Grimes," he says, heading for her, "you think I should start mopping up in front?" She nods sort of distractedly. Louise giggles. The grin on Jenny's face. You can imagine.

And there's worse. Because what Jenny told me yesterday—it didn't really register. But here she slips out the door with Louise and a couple other girls. And then I know. And suddenly I guess that everybody knows. The others, the ones who haven't left yet, they're wiping down the tables, changing clothes, whatever, none of them looking at me but not because of the usual reason. They're grinning. They think it's a stitch. Up from the ache in my legs and back swoops enough anger that my heart's pounding like in Jenny's bed. Where I can't be.

※

Two weeks it goes on this way, and no one's smiling anymore. Except maybe Lucille Grimes. The work's been good for her, just like her reverend said. She's so damn *pleasant*—everyone else is sullen. But the place is clean, cleaner than it's ever been. She's responsible in her own sneaky way. Whenever things are slow she'll take up a mop or wet rag and set to. But before she's made two passes one of the boys will trudge out from back. "Here, let me do that, Miss Grimes." Like his mamma just slapped him top of the head. How can I complain? I've been keeping to the back myself, busy at my desk with orders and schedules and the like.

Loneliness I'm used to. Been used to all my life. It's not people in general I miss. But, Lord, I miss Jenny—more than I could ever have guessed. I've never needed anyone and it's not that I *need* her. I miss the sweet spice smell of her. Out front she's worse than a stranger—an employee. But every now and then her eyes will dart my way, sorry and lonely too and angry, like it's all my fault—and hopeless because there's nothing to do, nothing she'll let me do.

It's the lull we get after lunch before the new shift arrives. At my desk there's nothing to do but wish I could get my legs in the air the way that helps. And there goes somebody yelling out front. Angry shouts are nothing new, and when I first hear them I'm not much for moving. Then I hear Lucy Grimes. That does the trick.

"Well, I *am* sorry—I don't know what I could have done with it."

"That's your problem, ain't it? We got *food* coming."

Five bucks over from where they're putting in a new motel. Young, black, trouble if you don't handle 'em right. Takes me maybe five seconds to see what she's done—lost the ticket with their order and they've already paid. Takes them maybe two seconds more to see they can push her. One up front in a fish-net shirt, baseball cap pulled round brim-back, is doing the pushing. Four behind him do harmony.

"What is this?—I got another cheeseburger coming," crows the lead.

"Fries too, couple orders of fries." This from the chorus. "And cokes—you forgot the cokes."

Lucy Grimes checks my way. She's confused and she's angry. My lips, tongue, jaw feel lead-heavy. I don't move. I don't say anything. She's squirming for sure. She fetches cheeseburger and fries, sets them carefully on the heap. Needs another tray for the cokes. Everybody's watching now— a couple other customers, all the help, and I can feel Jenny's watching me.

I'm watching me too—it's a real rush. I could stop it all quick enough, but I don't. All my life I've been baited and they're baiting her, toying, laughing, dancing through her humiliation. I'm talking to her without saying a word—This is what it's all about, feel it, taste it. Now you know. I feel the heat in my cheeks and throat. No ache in my back now. What's funny is that, even while I'm letting it happen and loving it, it's hurting me too, making me ashamed. I'm telling myself that it's wrong and not doing anything is about the worst thing you've ever done because you know it.

Louise is hiding her grin. The boys in back have their heads up over the racks where they can see and they aren't hiding anything. Carnival. And I'm not moving.

"Come on now, girl—you forgot my friend Jesse's hot dog," says the one. "That's right," say the others.

The muscles in Lucy's face and jaw jut tight—not a quiver, but tears have started, washing down heavy, and you can tell it's all she can do to stand there rigid. The bucks wear sassy grins, still waiting.

"You got what you're gonna get—get the hell out of here," says Jenny with a hot, quiet violence, pushing by me from her end of the counter. The grins aren't so sure now. All five of them glance from Jenny to me—I wave them out with a thumb.

"Anything you say, Mamma," the leader crows. Two of them grab the trays; two more jerk thumbs at me and hunch up a shoulder. Then they strut, the five of them, to a table outside by the parking lot.

Inside it's gone quiet. Embarrassed now that it's over, the other customers drift on their way. Louise already has the boys back to work. She's wiping and stacking clean trays herself. Except for wiping her eyes with a napkin, Lucy Grimes hasn't moved—she's staring out, shell-shocked, as if she hasn't really taken in what happened. She looks very young. Jenny's come to her side, takes her arm—grips tight because Lucy gives a surprised little squeal and jerks free.

"You happy now, Sister?" Jenny says. "Work been good for you? Loads of fun, ain't it—well you just keep having your fun." It's not my Jenny who spins away from Lucy Grimes—her face dark fury, her eyes blistering me, eye to eye. "You, you bastard." She's panting, hissing between tight teeth. "You should know and you're a bastard for it."

What can I say? What right's she got? I'll be damned if I'll give her the satisfaction. I shrug and stare right past her. But she's not waiting for anything—fetches her bag and charges out the door. Anyway, it's the end of the shift. I've got to get off my feet, aching from heels up into my neck. I know the headache that's gonna blind me next. Fuck them all.

❋

Now you got to give Lucy Grimes her due. Come five-thirty a.m. she's waiting for me with the others in the parking lot. They're a sleepy bunch, this crew, all relaxed in a way I haven't seen for a while, Lucy prissy and neat and not at all apart from the rest.

No surprise Jenny's not here. Better believe I don't need her.

A Dancer

Ariel Abrams was a small boy with startling blue eyes. They were unlike anyone else's eyes as far back as could be remembered on either side of the family. The mystery delighted his mother Sarah and vaguely embarrassed Harry Abrams. And the little boy did disconcert people, the way he stared at them with undisguised curiosity or, worse, out beyond them as if they were mere intervening figures on the landscape.

A secret about Ariel: he danced. Up he'd clamber onto his feet, leaning an arm against a wooden chair or table-leg, and swing his other arm as Sarah sang songs in the kitchen. And soon, soon as he could stand free, he raised both arms above his head and spun oh so slowly in little circles on the floor, singing *la la la* to all the world. How he fidgeted, wanting only to return to the dance, when Sarah swept him up in her arms and twirled in a bigger circle, she at the center, eyes closed tight as she gloried in this gift of joy.

On a summer afternoon, Harry might hoist Ariel on his shoulders and carry him down to the old carriage house. There the boy took his place on a horsehair sofa while Pop read aloud from a tattered Walter Scott.

Or they lit out into the piedmont, the paths cool in early

morning, Harry walking slow, Ariel trundling along quick as he could. Harry might take off his boots and wade a stream. Ariel, for his part, danced across the stone-mottled shallows, bobbed from one foot to the other with a gay splash and twisting leap, his face alight. He could dance the marrow-deep ache right out of Harry's wounded arm and chase the dark brooding that often attended it. Yet this dancing did at times vaguely embarrass his father as well, as if Ariel were truly a gift, a changeling who didn't entirely belong to them.

*

In the town where Ariel grew up there was a little synagogue shaped like a church. No one knew why this was so—whether it had once been the fashion or merely the expression of a desire not to stand out, not to stand apart. For a community of Jews had belonged to this town a very long time, and their little redbrick synagogue was well over a hundred years old by the time Ariel was born. Its roof peaked gracefully. Its arched windows shone with stained glass. There was, of course, no steeple.

Harry Abrams had years ago restored an old carriage-house just off Court Square. Out of it he ran a business in second-hand furniture and antique books. Trouble was, Harry became attached to his stock in the small shop. As customers browsed, he'd stand aside, filling the air with pipe smoke and shrouded far-away looks while Ariel slipped and darted through a broken reef of bookcases, sofas, shards of china.

Ariel's mother Sarah had been a newcomer to the town: met, wooed, and married by Harry while he was stationed in Baltimore. And not long afterwards, Harry off to the fight in Italy and Ariel already more than a glimmer, the war was preparing to cast up on the town another new arrival, a Miss Ruth Mendelsohn. Two of Ruth's aunts who lived in the town had beckoned to her from across the sea. They cabled money to intermediaries and messages and more money, and swept Ruth clear of Europe when it already seemed too late. And as this considerable feat was in its last stages, these two aunts, Sophie and Bessie Mendelsohn, proceeded to die, one within weeks of the other. Miss Ruth stepped ashore with one suitcase, and found waiting for her only what little money her aunts had left after the expenses of rescuing her and of their own modest funerals.

Sophie and Bessie, who were also aunts by blood or tradition to most every Jew in town, and not a few Gentiles, had not operated in secret, however. Now that they were gone, the community assumed responsibility for welcoming Ruth Mendelsohn into the family and for helping her on her feet. Harry Abrams, himself home from the war by this time with a crippled arm, had put most of the arrangements in place by the time Miss Ruth arrived. He and Sarah rode the Crescent up to New York to fetch the refugee home. They found a woman younger rather than older, wearing a mannish overcoat and heavy dark shoes, the kind hospital matrons wore. She looked a bit dazed, Miss Ruth did, and Harry and Sarah, catching a glimpse of tell-tale ankles and wrists, glanced at each other and didn't sigh out loud.

For the time being Miss Ruth was to have a place at their house. Every few days, not to over-do it, friends dropped round for tea or dinner. The idea was to introduce her gradually to the larger family. During these calls, she would sit quietly rocking in a rocking-chair. Sometimes Ariel climbed up into her lap and they would rock, the two of them, without a word or a thought for anyone else.

Miss Ruth's cheeks had very soon plumped up pink and healthy above a modest chin and a jaw that had a tendency to go slack. Her eyes were a blanched, nearly colorless blue. On she'd rock, smiling a calm far-away little smile while conversation swelled lightly around her. Of course everyone understood—allowance upon allowance had to be made for all she must have been through—it frightened them to imagine. It took some little while, therefore, before Harry and Sarah began to suspect that

Miss Ruth was a bit simple, and a while longer before they confessed their suspicions to each other.

Mind you, not that she was incapacitated. Ruth even spoke a schoolgirl's English. "Thank you very kindly for toast," she'd chirp, as if in recalling her vocabulary lessons she had also to recall the girlish pitch of her own youth, while gazing at Sarah earnestly. Yet when conversation grew ever so slightly abstract—about why the price of eggs had soared or why it might be that Ariel was somewhat tardy in learning to speak—a look of contented distraction appeared on Miss Ruth's face.

After what had grown to a number of months with the Abrams, she moved to a pleasant boarding house along the same street. Her meals she took with the landlady, Mrs. Padnos. It was never apparent to Miss Ruth that the small income from her aunts' bequest wasn't nearly enough to cover expenses. But Mrs. Padnos knew whom to visit with a plain piece of paper marked neatly in pencil. Miss Ruth was, after all, simple. And as they would have done in Eastern Europe, had there been any Jews remaining in Eastern Europe, the community looked on this as a special claim; they continued what they'd begun, sharing responsibility for Ruth Mendelsohn.

✳

One day when Ariel was four, another boy from all of a block and a half away ventured down the sidewalk. This other boy was a year older than Ariel and he was a bully. Every so often he'd catch Ariel playing on the grass in front of the house and taunt him from a little ways away. "Dance, dance, like a girl," he'd cry. And Ariel, who was remarkably self-possessed, ignored this would-be tormentor and continued his play to the strange music of the taunts themselves.

On this one particular day, however, the other boy had learned something new. "*Jooboy.* Go ahead and dance like a girl, jooboy," he sang. Inside the house Harry and Sarah heard the cries and hurried to the screen door. Sarah caught Harry by the sleeve. "Wait," she said. A few feet away Miss Ruth sat quietly in her chair, stiff and attentive, not rocking.

This time Ariel faced the other boy. He was very serious and he was very upset. His face was dark with fury, his eyes flushed already with tears. The bully, amazed perhaps at such unexpected success, paused for a long moment. Then he shouted it aloud again. "Go ahead, why don't you dance, jooboy?"

Ariel, serious as could be, stooped to the ground and tore off a fistful of grass. He stood, solemnly lifted his arm, and hurled the green blades into the air. "*I throw grass at you*," he cried furiously in his turn.

Stunned and amazed, mystified and alarmed, the bully's eyes filled with tears of their own. He spun round and fled away home. Ariel watched him go and after a little while, sad, he sat down in the grass.

The screen door slapped. Down the steps, gripping the rail for support, came Miss Ruth. She said nothing. Her eyes were watery behind the thick lenses, her face flushed. She settled herself down awkwardly not far from Ariel and uprooted one fistful of grass after another and sprinkled the blades and dirt into her wide lap.

※

When time came for school, Ariel played kickball during recess with his classmates. He'd take his turn kicking or catching a ball, watching his teammates and watching himself too. It left a hollow place deep inside him. For their part, the other boys treated him as an outsider, some of them because he was a Jew, some because they thought he thought he was too good for them, some because he seemed to want it that way. There'd be days when he'd walk right off the field in the middle of a game and find a sheltered place by the wire fence until recess was over. It was things like that that got him in trouble—

his teammates screeched, the other team hooted, and next time he might not be picked at all.

The secret of his dancing he kept largely to himself. Twice a week Sarah met him out front of the school, Miss Ruth often beside her on the front seat of the Studebaker. Across town at Blair Elementary, Ariel could dance—the only boy among seventeen dancers in the class—and not risk teasing by kids from his own school.

There were problems enough, of course. Some of the girls resented the intruder. Others teased him for not being much of a boy, though he wore sweatpants instead of a leotard. And Miss Darcy, the instructor, she didn't know what to do with the quiet boy with those blue eyes. He was a promising dancer, yet *dreamy*.

Once the music on the phonograph began—even during warmups and routine drill—Ariel could close his eyes and lose himself. He'd be standing there against the rail, cold and bored, or watching one or another of the girls who might make him shiver if she happened to glance his way and smile. He bobbed up and down on his toes, absently at first. Back deep in his calf, down low, he felt the first snap and pulse, yes, spreading like flame. Dancing, with a partner or not, he'd be alone—a solitude different than other times and not so lonely, alone and yet, caught up in the dance, connected to all the world.

*

Another day of chauffeuring was added to Sarah's schedule when Ariel turned nine. On Wednesday afternoons now, as well as Tuesdays and Thursdays, she and Miss Ruth drove him over to Blair Elementary, though not to dance. In recent years a number of Jewish families, along with many others, had moved to the growing town. With eight or ten students to make it worthwhile, a young teacher, himself new to the area, was now offering private Hebrew lessons at Blair.

Sarah was soon able to share this particular duty with a friend, Maryanne Malakar, whose family was one of those recently arrived. Her son, Anthony, a good two years older than Ariel, also began to make the short trip cross town. The two boys might have been taken for brothers, were Anthony not dark enough to be Ariel's shadow. Once a week, in Sarah's old Studebaker or Maryanne's new Lincoln, the boys traveled together, shrieking their new Hebrew chants out the windows.

Other than on these weekly forays, however, they rarely spent time together. Ariel was somewhat awed by the older boy, Anthony Malakar. A little intimidated, a little disturbed. For Anthony had a smile that was full of magic. He'd cock his head, eyes narrow and knowing and wry. Dark as a gypsy, fine-boned without a hint of anything feminine, Anthony was neither shy nor self-conscious. He was very popular. The fact that he was a Jew bothered him not at all. Ariel Abrams watched this dark and magic boy from a distance.

At twelve Anthony Malakar was already something for the girls, though he'd have nothing to do with them at school. No, there he'd be alone at the center of a crowd of boys, unmindful of them all, laughing offhandedly or sharing a sly secret with his cousin Ned, who visited regularly from the north. (Ned had a toothy leer, his skin already deeply pocked by acne. Yet his cousin Anthony granted him a privileged intimacy.) Anthony dressed with infinite carelessness and a considerable style that the other boys copied quick as they could—and the very effort set them apart. The girls watched him.

❋

Half a dozen delicate silver bracelets jangled on Mrs. Malakar's arm as she struck a match for the sabbath candles, and Ariel thought it was silly, the solemn pout she wore while doing it. Max Malakar, a dark bearish little man, blessed the wine in a quick growl without chanting, as if this were a prank from a long time ago that still embarrassed him.

With a gesture Sarah Abrams became herself again, at least to Ariel's eyes. She was ladling peas onto Miss Ruth's plate and, as automatic as buttering bread, used her own knife to slice some of the chicken off the drumstick on her friend's plate. There was something about the cock of her elbows as she did this, efficient, graceful, and thoughtless, that almost made up for the rest of it, for her trying so hard to be sophisticated, to show Maryanne Malakar and her husband that she came from a good family in Baltimore and knew how things should be done—the way she held herself stiff, as if the chair was soiled and she didn't dare lean back. Not that Pop didn't embarrass him too, and Miss Ruth.

Even before Mama had finished cutting chicken from the bone to help her, Miss Ruth began mixing mashed potatoes and peas together and spooning them greedily into her mouth. Ariel ached with shame. She didn't close her mouth when she chewed, hunching over the plate with such undisguised pleasure. Her elbows dimpled she was so heavy, and her slate grey hair, which Mrs. Padnos chopped short like a boy's, was never quite clean. He knew she smelled funny too, musty. And she was *his* Miss Ruth, as far as Anthony Malakar was concerned.

They'd all come to the Malakars' for Friday dinner. Afterwards the grownups were going to drop Miss Ruth off and then go on themselves. As a hostage to the affection between his mother and Maryanne Malakar, Ariel was to stay here overnight with Anthony and his cousin Ned. He'd been dreading the evening. Yet secretly—he couldn't entirely deny it to himself—a certain thrill of anticipation for what might come later made his legs pump nervously. If Anthony felt like talking, sharing the secrets he knew, Ariel might learn what it meant to be nearly thirteen instead of ten. He wanted desperately to know. If only he knew, perhaps he wouldn't always feel such an outsider.

Here at their end of the dining room table, as Ariel writhed, Anthony and Ned were observing the visitors and flashing secret little glances and smiles to each other, not even caring that Ariel could see. And he did see. They paid especial attention to Miss Ruth. For Anthony's benefit, and no doubt for Ariel's, Ned lifted a fork and, with the slightest of stabs at a pea, mimicked her, a flash of mirth in his eye that seemed wicked and no less than the witness of truth itself.

But why did Mama have to fuss over these people—Mr. Malakar, who didn't really close his mouth when he chewed either. Maryanne Malakar with her bony, furtive fingers and her silly giggle when she was trying to please Mama. Couldn't they see what he saw—what all the kids at school saw—that Anthony was the one who mattered, the one who carried it off, the one who knew the secrets? How coarse Anthony's parents seemed in comparison!

Just sitting here, an audience to this dark boy mocking them all, made Ariel long more than ever to be in his confidence. And yet at the root of his tongue he tasted something cold and tarnished. The enchanting slit of Anthony's delicate eye repelled him and held him fast. He wasn't sure what it was about the way Anthony carried himself; it had something to do with money and something to do with arrogance, but was more. It was in his elegant slouch and the cock of his head. The dark coy glance up from under. But it was really deep in his eyes themselves, a teasing, knowing look, scorning any other knowledge. It took Ariel's breath away. It scared him and, oh, how he yearned for a peek at it. Anthony could mock because he *knew*, and neither his own parents nor Ariel's could ever fathom it.

❋

"That auntie of yours sure is a doll, Ariel—one pretty lady." The words drifted like smoke through the darkness, caressed with Ned's affected drawl.

"She's *not*—not my aunt," snapped Ariel, hating Ned and hating the squeak of his own voice and feeling that he'd already done something shameful.

"Ah, of course not—my mistake," said Ned. The sneer might as well have been visible.

"Now, Ned, cut it out. My friend Ariel wouldn't lie. She's really not his aunt. Or she's his aunt and everybody else's at the same time." Anthony lay with his hands behind his head, musing it through aloud. Ariel could just make out his shape in the darkness. "We're all supposed to look after her—aren't we, Ariel? She's your aunt and my aunt, all one big family. You hear that, Ned?"

Ned snorted. "She may be yours, not mine, Cousin. No way I've got any aunt who's so dumb and so ugly."

"Boy, you are one stupid shit," said Anthony slowly and decisively. There was no answer, but Ariel, who lay on the guest cot while the others shared the room's big bed, saw Ned rise up on an elbow beyond Anthony. In the shadows his acne scarred face seemed twisted into a grinning mask.

Anthony began to speak again, but his voice had changed, grown sing-song as he told them a tale. "She wasn't always this way, you know. You should have seen her as a girl."

"Yeah," Ned interrupted. "She was young a million years ago. Younger and still stupid and ugly."

Oh, Ariel hated him—*hated* him. He wanted to hear more, for Anthony to go on. Already the dance of the older boy's voice made him shiver.

"No, no," came the gentle croon, dismissing the coarseness of such an image. "No, she was young, and she was so beautiful when it happened." ("*What?*" whispered Ned and Ariel together.) Anthony hesitated as if he were squinting, trying to make the story out. "She would have been maybe your age, right, Ariel? Not even any hair down below, or maybe the lightest little bit. And such small, small breasts." ("Call 'em *tits*, why don't you," murmured Ned.) Anthony laughed a far away laugh, enchanted with the image he was creating.

Ariel lay tense, glimpsing the promised magic. Because the story was Anthony's, it was potent beyond measure.

"So she's beautiful and young, and she's pure as a virgin." Ned was coaxing and wheedling now, unable to resist mimicking the chant with a faint sarcastic burr of his own, yet intent on drawing Anthony out, for he was excited too.

"She is a virgin."

"AN-THON-Y," sang Ned, "she's probably still one--what changed her from this princess of yours into such a witch?"

Almost no pause this time. Anthony was piecing the story together to the same rhythm he was telling it. "The big bad wolves got her, boy—those Nazis did it to her. She grew up over there and only got away free afterwards."

Stop, thought Ariel.

"I thought they just killed 'em."

"Most. But some, some who were young and beautiful and who they'd do things to, they let 'em go afterwards."

Stop, Ariel pleaded silently, the magic turning nasty.

"Ah," whispered Ned, his voice flush with a breathless ache.

"Oh, yes." Anthony, lying hands behind his head, chanted the tale to the darkness and silence and waiting ears. "They did things to her, hurt her, things you'd do to a girl like that, slowly and for a long time, so when it's over there's no need to say anything anymore, and you're not young and beautiful anymore.

"Maybe they all did it to her, one after another—think of it. Maybe she even liked it. Think of it. Maybe they'd scratch her, not deep, just for the taste of it. Or burn her, maybe with cigarettes, against her white skin. Just think."

"Oh shit, don't stop," Ned panted.

Anthony didn't stop. On and on the story went. And as Anthony followed where the tale led him, Ariel stared up towards the ceiling, horror crawling dead-cold along his belly and spine.

He was afraid to close his eyes for what he might see without any light at all. His throat was dry, his heart pounding. The story had turned a hidden corner and revealed a door Ariel had never guessed was there—or it had been there all along and sealed tight by silent conspiracy. It seemed to him as he lay in the darkness that the subject, the questions, the not-daring-to-know had been hidden away by his family, by everyone, for so long that they'd almost been forgotten. But now that door stood gaping ajar. And what scared Ariel most of all was the queer sensation that he'd peeked here before, unremembered. Anthony Malakar was reciting a tale that rang deep and familiar. Ariel shouldn't have listened, shouldn't have heard, but now he'd heard and if it made him sick it excited him too.

✳

Much later in the night, when the cousins were long asleep, Ariel Abrams snuck out of the Malakar house and wandered towards the heart of town. A hound woke in its pen as he passed an alley. It barked feebly, snuffled, and slept again. Court Square loomed ahead, ghostly, neither dark nor light in the moonlight. He knew his way, knew every step, every locust tree and red brick. Yet tonight the high moon had blanched all life and color from the earth, and the brick glimmered grey. None of the buildings and trees, not even the great equestrian Lee himself, possessed any substance at all.

Ariel had no specific goal in mind. What he wanted was to walk until he could not walk any more, to keep breathing in as much air as his lungs would hold. He wanted to crawl into bed between his parents, to smell their warm sleep smell, to be held and caressed for no reason.

As he walked, Miss Ruth's face floated in and out of his thoughts, flushing him with fleeting snatches of disgust and affection, all haunted with echoes of Anthony's chant. A young girl, naked and vulnerable, a silent "oh" on her lips, chased after

Miss Ruth. Shaking his head again and again didn't clear it of dreams and images that left no room for breath. Ariel panted and hurried on nowhere.

Moon or no moon, the town hardly seemed real to him, he or it or both of them disembodied and no part of each other.

The ashes in his mouth were the end of Anthony's magic. He knew the other boy's spell would never capture him again. But Ariel, now that it was too late not to know, felt soiled, the last gift of magic.

A couple of blocks from the old courthouse, sharp against the night sky, arched the roof of the little synagogue. With a snort, contemptuous of it and of himself, Ariel drifted that way.

Ignoring the low iron gate, he slipped past a hedge and into the yard. He stared up at the synagogue as if he'd never quite seen it before. It seemed so small, a stage-prop or a joke, costumed like a church, an embarrassing fraud he'd only just learned to recognize. The high windows were blank in the night.

In a few hours, come Saturday morning, his parents would stroll up the hill from the other side of the square. Along the way they'd stop at the boarding house to fetch Miss Ruth along if she wished. Ariel snorted again.

Ariel Abrams stood in the moonlight, hugging himself. He was hugging himself, chin pressed again his chest. He swayed from one leg to the other and back. He swayed and circled slow in front of the synagogue. And he was dancing without intending it, to no music in the quiet night. He danced ever so slowly, his arms crossed tight around his body, only his legs moving. It was a dreamy dance. It felt good to dance in the moonlight and against the motion of the earth, dancing to clear his mind and cleanse his soul of Anthony Malakar's magic.

Hard Feelings

Guido wanders back from the john, changed, his eyes lit up out of focus, his smile out of kilter under the wispy blond mustache. He looks just like one of these christmas-tree geese he's been folding for me out of cocktail napkins—something from nothing, shapes you recognize, yet strange too. *Jesus*, I think, *wouldn't you know?*

If there'd been any guessing it was one of those nights when a few beers set him off, I'd never let him bring me. But you can't tell when it'll happen with Guido, and it don't except every now and then.

"Anyone who votes Republican is a whore," he says loud and triumphant, wearing this holy grin like he's found the Truth scribbled back there in the john.

Jeremy, behind the bar, glances over quick and sharp, sees what I see, makes a face. He's known Guido long as any of us, and this is the last thing he needs early on a Saturday night. If the well-off types who cruise out this way from the city to slum and eat chili and burgers, if they see too much hassle, they're liable to hit the road again and keep driving out the river. Can't say *I'd* miss them any, but the people Jeremy and his daddy owe money to surely would.

"Anyone votes anyhow in this day and age is a whore," Guido barks defiantly. Suddenly (and this is Guido) his eyes go soft and runny like an underdone egg. "None of them politicians, not one of them, knows what it's like."

I'm thinking, what is he *on* about? Did someone leave a scrap of newspaper in the stall?

A couple of girls in booths along the wall take a peek to see what's up. But so far their boys and the ones at the bar, most of them local boys this early, just tighten their jaws and take a pull at whatever's in front of them. Me, I'm not going to coax him back, not this time. Wouldn't do any good. I'm sitting in our booth with the paper goose he's made for me, and I'm taking out the folds one at a time, smoothing them hard with the palm of my hand, turning that poor little goose back into a cocktail napkin.

"Look at welfare," cries Guido. "You think that does poor people any good?—Not on your life it doesn't. Don't even get to the ones who need it. It's a shitty joke. And here's these damn Republicans trying to get rid of the whole damn thing, damn their asses." His adams-apple is bobbing the length of his scrawny neck.

Just what we all want to hear too, as if everybody out here's taking stamps and handouts. Certainly not Guido, not with what carpenters make. Where does he get off making it political, shaming people if they take stamps? I'm cursing him good now, and cursing myself for letting him coax me into this when I *know* better.

One thing I've never known, strange as it may be, is where the *Guido* comes from. I mean, his real name's odd enough—Everett. Everett Cockerell. Ev. But in our town this five-foot-seven spindly man's been called Guido since we were kids. One of life's mysteries.

Another mystery is why he goes off this way without warning, like a switch's gone click in his head. It's not just the beer—hard to tell whether the beer triggers the mood or the mood sets him off drinking. Either way, booze is a handy excuse.

He's over at the end of the bar, shouting and mumbling and not making much sense and stomping his foot for attention. From what I can tell, Jeremy's about had it already. He's changing a keg and not looking at Guido only two feet away. But the scowl he's wearing is dangerous. Maybe Guido sees, maybe not, but he sure don't care.

For my part I'm ignoring Guido too. Never seen the loon before.

He's such a quiet, gentle guy most of the time. A carpenter. Usually it's only his hands that talk. They're quick and sure, quick and alive. Like the way they work pure magic folding paper. More than once I've thought about how those hands would know, all on their own, the way to map every inch of a woman. But you'd never find out. He'd figure something had to be said first and then never get it out, stammering even with people he's known all his life. My first husband should have been so shy.

So how come this jerk who's so sensitive is picking a fight with no one in particular in Jake's? (Jake is Jeremy's dad.) Guido's cozied up to one of the visitors—this one unusual for driving out to the sticks all by himself. He's wearing jeans that are ironed and red loafers with the little tassels on them. Someone must have told him about Jeremy's burgers. As a matter of fact, he's doing his best to put one away right now, except that Guido's perched at his ear, whispering I can just imagine what, though the guy has the burger in both hands and he's chewing away at it, head down, as if Guido isn't there.

Back when we were kids in school, Guido used to make me gifts. There's no denying he had a crush. Of course he'd never just come out and hand me something—the tension would have killed him. But I'd discover the stuff anywhere, anytime. A pencil sketch of a tree or a teacher or of me, wedged into my notebook. A clay ashtray from workshop. Best of all, these animals he whittled from a block of scrap wood. Deer, fish, a pretty incredible blue jay. They'd ride smooth and kind of heavy in your hand. When no one was looking I'd close my eyes and trace my fingers like a blind person reading them, across their eyes and mouths and along the cool, smooth ridge of their backs.

So I felt bad when I had to get rid of them and I felt sorry for Guido. The gifts that would burn I burned in an old barbecue grate at the park where nobody would be. That seemed better somehow than just chucking them out. We were fifteen then, and some of my friends were already getting married, having kids even, and the last thing in the world I needed at fifteen was for people to see me holding onto gifts from Guido. It wasn't bad that he gave them to me—being worshiped is good for your image—I just couldn't be caught keeping them.

Jeremy must be crazy himself, giving him another beer. Probably thinks that will shut him up. Fat chance. Not once one of these fits of feeling has welled up.

Guido's always had too many feelings rumbling around inside him without any safety valve to ease them off. You'd think people that quiet wouldn't get upset or at least wouldn't need to show it this way. And most of the time that's Guido—gentle as a lamb and the best listener I've ever talked to. He's sat up with me through the bad times and listened. Listened when all I needed was for someone to sit there and hear me out and feel sorry—but not say anything, for chrisake.

Then there are the other times, once in a blue moon, when his feelings just take and run with him and make him crazy.

What that brings to mind is Lucy Chamberlin getting herself knocked up. We were juniors in school. Amazing that most every girl could know about it and not a soul else, not even the jerk who couldn't manage a rubber. Lucy was about the cutest girl ever, with her little tennis sneakers and short white socks. And she wasn't about to screw up all her fun by dropping a kid so early.

Her cousin Maggie was a couple years older, and a lot older than that in other ways. Maggie got her boyfriend to give her a lift into the city, and back she comes with a gift for Lucy—a magic potion that's supposed to do its job without you traveling anywhere. I thought it sounded pretty suspicious at the time. But it worked, yes sir. Not two days later Lucy lost her little package.

Course she wound up in the hospital herself, nip and tuck for a month and came back to school looking a zillion years old and those little tennis shoes doing her no good at all anymore.

But first of all before that something had to be done with her little package. There wasn't a lot of time or opportunity, and it got us, those Maggie suckered to help, feeling pretty squeamish. What were we supposed to do? Why'd it take more than Maggie anyway? The thing was wrapped in an old bedspread (I never brought myself to peek inside), and we laid it carefully at the bottom of a bin that would be loaded and emptied with a lot of other trash from the lumber yard. I even started to whisper the only prayer I could remember (now I lay me) with Maggie and Alice Perkins joining in, when we heard someone coming and away we ran and hid. And who's the someone but Guido, poking through here for wood scraps from the lumber yard. Which I might possibly have remembered he did on Saturdays if there'd been time to think of anything.

Only Guido would have this kind of luck. Not just to look in the bin and see the bedspread but to get curious and poke at it with a strip of molding. I was set for him to get sick—which he did after a second or two of surprise and not-believing, hunched and jerking his lungs. Not a sound from him, not a sound all the while. But Alice and Maggie, it's all I can do to keep them quiet cause they're shaking with giggles.

What's he gonna do, call the sheriff? No, Guido (did he already have that wispy mustache?) does what we should have done, would have done if we'd only thought. He lifts the package out and carries it back behind those bins into the wide sandy bank just above the river and scoops out a hole with a jagged-edged piece of scrap. He's careful, neat. Into the hole he lays Lucy's mistake gently as can be and tucks it under the covers of sand and dirt and even a little wild grass, patting the mound that's like a girl's belly.

At the time I thought that was the end of it. As soon as the coast was clear, the three of us girls snuck off to Alice's house and borrowed some of her daddy's whiskey. We'd earned it. It wasn't til Monday I heard about Guido drifting down to the American Legion field that p.m. already drunk off his head and cussing both teams up a storm. (Where he'd got hold of the corn whiskey, nasty raw stuff, I don't know). Next thing you know he's slipped a brand new bat out of a duffle and starts whacking at the backstop hard as he can. It surprised me he'd do that, mangle any good piece of wood. Anyway, the team did pretty much the same to his face—it was purple and black for weeks.

Maybe he'd gone off crazy like that before, but it was the first I heard of it.

He's been away at the can again and now he slams back into the bar. "Toilet seat's broke," he announces. "You ought to buy better quality, Jeremy. But I can fix it for you Monday. No charge." He's wearing a silly grin that's bashful and guilty and cocky as all get out.

"Shut up, okay Guido?" says Jeremy.

"Sure. Damn right I'll shut up. Put a muzzle on me cause I'm telling the truth, always the truth and nothin' but the truth. Last thing I want to do is embarrass my friend Jeremy and cost him business."

Drunk is drunk and there's nothing charming to him right now. He's like every other drunk in the world. Boring. Do they ever know it? Never. And that only makes them more boring. I'm sitting there in the booth while all this is going on, my plate of nachos wiped clean, and I'm sipping at my own beer. I may have to listen but I don't have to look. I don't know why I let him bring me in the first place, but nobody who wasn't there to see us arrive needs ever know.

"Jesus, Jeremy—all I want's another Rolling Rock." He's laid an arm on the shoulder of the same paying customer he was hassling before like he's some piece of the furniture. The guy shrugs him clear once, only for Guido to poke his bony elbow right onto the exact same place on his neck. That's the end of it. Shrugging clear again, the stranger stands, throws a couple of bucks on the bar and stomps out of the place offended, like he's been dirtied or his expensive shirt's been wrinkled. Guido, naturally, doesn't so much as notice. "Quit making such a big deal, Jeremy. Just one more."

"Shut up, Guido. No more."

"Why're you being such a bastard? Just give me a beer and I'll be good."

"You'll be nothing," Jeremy says, quiet and not looking at him, which Guido ought to know how to read. "Get out of here, Guido. Don't say another word—no, shut up, not a one. Right now, outta here."

"Shit," he whines. But his shoulders sag. He looks like he's ready to start crying. Too much feeling again. That's his curse. I know for a fact he hasn't forgotten me back in the booth, but he pretends to. Won't even glance round as he slouches out the screen door.

It's not five minutes, though, before we hear him again. He's abusing the eight or ten people who've carried food out to the picnic tables off the parking lot. It was their choice to go out there and no one's serving them except what they come in to get, so Jeremy's not going to worry about Guido anymore. That's when I'm thinking, *Neither am I.*

Pretty soon we're hearing something we didn't inside the bar—angry voices answering Guido. I can't make out the words, but it's nasty enough I don't need to. I swing out of the booth and back in the other side so I can get a look out the door. All there's to see is a pudgy girl with long stringy hair, bare feet, and a pink-terry tank-top, sitting on one of the benches. A helmet's lying on the ground beside. Jeannie Paynter's lips are moving but she's not saying anything—or I can't hear it—her heels are pumping up and down in the dirt and she's clapping her hands softly, nervously. Talk about a bad sign.

As soon as that registers, sure enough, who should waltz by the door—and that's a joke—but her old man, Brunstad? Now, Jeannie's maybe seventeen, eighteen, and doesn't look that old. Brunstad, he's our age and looks sixty and wasted, as if he's done every drug, every crime, every disease they've thought to invent. It only makes him meaner to see, hair wiped clean from the top of his head, long peppery strings left hanging around the sides, him standing about six-four and a gut spreading from here to tomorrow and knuckles that really ought to be scraping the gravel. Him we can hear, cursing Guido in a low growl, his turn to be saying shut your mouth.

"Fuck you," squeaks Guido off to the side and out of sight. "A man's got a right to say what he needs to say."

It'd help if some of it was worth the saying, I'm thinking, probably not alone.

Brunstad's crowd are *delighted*. They're revving with laughter and shouts, taunting Guido, chanting Brunstad on to his chores.

Brunstad passes by the doorway again. He's sort of ridiculous, the way he's gripping the little green beer bottle by the neck like he's in some bad movie. If I'm not moving now it's only because I'm frozen. Truth to tell, scared almost to wetting my pants.

"Jesus H. Christ," says Jeremy, finishing the draw on a beer from the tap and wiping his hands on a rag as he walks out into the lot. Him moving sets me free too and I slip out right behind.

Like some dog-and-bear act in a circus, Guido and Brunstad dance a little lumbering dance, circling each other and slowly drifting along the tilt of the bank down towards the river. Maybe finally and at last Guido's realized what he's got himself into. His skin isn't white so much as greenish-grey and he looks like all the beer in him isn't sitting too well. Finally and at last he's not saying anything either. But Brunstad is still talking to him, low and mean but sort of gentle too—he doesn't want to spook his catch.

I give Jeremy a shove in the arm but he shakes me off. He's got no taste for getting in the middle of this, not unless it's inside his damn bar. I give him another shove, a shot with both hands right in the kidney and it isn't to make him move but for its own sake.

I'm so furious with Jeremy that I catch only a green flash of the bottle. By the time I look, Guido's already bleeding from the raw purple gash above his ear, wobbling but still upright, dazed. But no one's looking at him because—and who can figure it?— untouched, Brunstad's sinking to his knees. It's ever so slow, like one of those sports films where you catch every twist and turn. Brunstad pauses kneeling in the dirt, might almost be a choir boy waiting for Sunday wafer and wine, before tipping forward onto one arm (one great paw of knuckles I should say) and glancing back over his shoulder at Jeannie Paynter, puzzled at what's happening. More than ever he looks like a great bear as his arm gives way and he rolls onto his side. The silence seems to come from the hammer that's not pounding in his chest, as if we'd been hearing it all along and never knew what we were hearing.

Only Jeannie's sudden wail shows how quiet it's become. Then all hell really does break loose. From going very slow, everything is happening very fast.

One of the city women darts forward and shoves Jeannie off of Brunstad (the girl is crying and wailing, her nose running, as she's held back by two other girls from the pack), rips his army-surplus shirt open, and starts pumping rhythmically. (Isn't she supposed to give mouth-to-mouth too)? From all the response she's getting, it's only a big slab of warm meat.

Jeremy's disappeared inside to the phone, and the rescue squad is damn impressive, shrieking along the highway in not much over two minutes, followed by a fire truck and another ambulance.

It's getting dark, and people are drifting in from all sides with the darkness. The whole town, it seems, come to pay respects to Brunstad.

No one gets too close, though. We're all still standing in the gravel drive. Brunstad's lying maybe fifteen yards down the bank. That woman from the city, a nurse or something, passes her place pumping to one of the boys on the rescue squad, who catches and doesn't miss a beat, while the rest of his crew heft Brunstad onto a stretcher and up towards one of the ambulances. Once they've got him inside—the pumping on his chest never so much as stuttering—they hook up wires and hoses, the latest stuff they've got, and I'm already pretty sure that if they're having to pump and stick needles in him at this stage, it's all for show.

Who's milling about meanwhile? Well, there's Jeannie Paynter, stunned, scared, not even crying now, wandering.

And then there's Guido. He's staggering about too. The left side of his head and face is streaked with blood from the gash, but the blood's dried and so has the wound and apparently it hasn't started to ache yet. He's scared too and puzzled—as if he can't quite figure what's happened. Lost soul. He needs some looking after. And I bet it's me he's looking for in a vague sort of way.

But I'm standing outside the rim of the crowd, off the gravel and in the darkness where I can see everything going on: the hospital-bright squinched insides of the ambulance, Jeremy bobbing and weaving under a heavy tray of beers for the crowd. (Hasn't done his business any harm after all). That's the problem really—too many people. That's what keeps me from going to Guido.

The new set of flashing lights, after the fire trucks and ambulance, are blue, two sets of them swinging into the lot. Just when people have begun to drift away again or to settle into their brews, this stirs up the excitement pretty good. The sheriff wanders through the crowd, saying hello, patting folks on the back. It's his deputy who keeps the notepad open as he tags behind. It doesn't take them long at all. What's to discover?

There's another fluster of excitement as one of the guys from the rescue squad reaches down for Jeannie's wrist and hauls her up into the ambulance for a ride.

So no one but me much notices when the sheriff gently leads Guido to the backseat of his car for a ride of his own. Maybe to the hospital too, to stitch up that gash. Poor Guido. Everett. Ev. With his luck they'll decide he's some uncontrollable brute who took Brunstad out on purpose.

The Excuse

Joshua she left on the narrow porch of the church and limped heavily into down nave, hunting me out. In her fist she was carrying a tight roll of dirty bills as if it were a lantern probing the darkness. A rough-hewn cane in her other hand swung ahead at every second step. Since I'd just emerged from the confessional, she found me easily enough.

"We got to talk," said Madelyn. Her cane poked the air. "You want to go back in there?"

"Only if you've got something to confess," I said. I spread my eyes wide, all innocence, teasing her. This time she was on my own territory and I was delighted.

"Not a thing I ain't proud of—but what I got to say is private," she declared with an arch glance over her shoulder at two outraged Armenian women who'd just finished, one after the other, minutely confessing their weighty sins. Yes, and they certainly did stare back at her, this enormous black woman past sixty, money still clutched in her fist.

"You'd better come back into the vestry," I said, and marched Madelyn away.

She limped into my study on her cane, only to wheel round once we'd crossed the threshold. "You got to go to the police and get old Abramson out," she said impatiently, as if we'd already been through this a dozen times. She shoved the money against my chest, but I fell farther back. "They ain't no rabbi here no more," she insisted, "so you got to get him."

My surprise and good humor at Madelyn's visit had by this time disappeared like so much smoke. Wary, baffled, I needed a moment to grasp what she was on about. "What's your Mr. Abramson done?"

"He took a poke with a gun at one of our boys. The boy Jamie's okay—just dumb. Only kid in the neighborhood dumb enough to get caught with candy bars up his coat by that old man. And then to start teasing and bragging about it and calling Abramson names. The boy ain't even scratched. But the police took Mr. Abramson downtown, maybe for his own good. Anyway, Mr. Priest, now you got to run on down and get him out."

I realized I'd been shaking my head and shaking my head, half in disbelief, half in protest. "You don't need me for that. I hardly know the man. Really, I'd be happy to—but I'm supposed to be hearing confessions all afternoon. Can't one of you take the bail down?"

"Can't, *Father*—he shot at one of our boys," Madelyn said, disgusted with such prevarication. "Now how would that look, us goin' down to rescue him? People talk enough as 'tis."

So what was I to do? Was I supposed to stand firm and refuse her? What kind of choice for a priest is that? Dutifully, Madelyn standing at my shoulder, I telephoned and spoke to a lieutenant at the precinct. Yes, they had Mr. Abramson—Would I come pick him up? The lieutenant sounded only too glad to hear from me. He figured an eighty-some-year-old man might not be entirely comfortable among their other guests.

Much as I hated driving, there was nothing to do but climb into the parish's brown boat of a Chrysler (eight months in this parish and I still hadn't mastered its column shift) and head towards the river.

My reluctance—not to mention surprise that Madelyn should make such a demand—stemmed, you see, from my single previous encounter with her Mr. Abramson. For it had hardly been a pleasant introduction, there in his grocery not three weeks earlier.

Our parish neighborhood—most of the city's older neighborhoods—are honeycombed with these markets. Like hermit crabs, many have adopted the shells of strategically placed old houses, their ground floors hollowed out and then crammed with hedgerows of cans and sacks and shelves. The big supermarket chains won't come into the area, you understand. No profits, they claim; too dangerous; shopping carts snatched all the time.

So groceries have become another bother for my parishioners, the ones who haven't yet moved out to the suburbs. Those who remain are still clustered together within a few blocks each way of St. Stephen's, in row houses where they've lived twenty, thirty years or more. Most of the men, at least those with seniority, have managed to hold onto jobs over at the Six Mile Ford plant. Their wives climb into cars and make suburban pilgrimages for groceries. But Blacks who live on every side haven't been in this neighborhood so long, don't have the jobs or the cars. The corner markets are for them.

Just about the same time that I was assigned to St. Stephen's, the church youth group joined up with Focus Health, a community organization concerned about the poor nutrition of local babies. Our kids, all twelve of them, were to visit local markets and discover what sorts of formula and baby food were available and at what price, compared to the supermarkets out in the suburbs.

Six or eight of the kids at a time went scouring the neighborhood, checking off markets from a master-list the Focus Health people had provided. Each Saturday morning they traveled out on foot; what trouble could there be? No trouble at all on the first two trips, aside from scowling men at the cash registers. Come the third Saturday, however, they were challenged by the manager at one grocery. Who you doing this for? he demanded. Father Libberdi, they chose to say. He's a prostitute, the manager said.

"He called you a prostitute," Michael Trgovic, the sixteen-year-old president of the youth group, reported to me later that morning in the vestry. The twelve-year-old Geiger twins giggled. I sinned in thought.

Thereafter, on Saturday mornings for a month, I went traipsing along on their rounds. Full November, mind you—wind and sleet hurling in from the river. We'd arrive at a market and be allowed in without much fuss, everyone on good behavior, youth group and management, me huddling as inconspicuously as possible by the coal stove or kerosene heater, smiling. The boys up by the registers were white and cool and tough. The men in charge, the managers, weren't so young or cool. In fact, not a few of them were parishoners, ever so polite to me. (Come next morning I'd be distributing wine and wafers to their wives).

It didn't take more than a couple of weeks for us to realize that mom and pop had precious little to do with these markets. Or that a fair bit of cash could be turned over, what with a captive clientele and no real competition. Different members of the same small pool of management would circle ahead of us, anticipating the bases we were to touch. It seemed they had one of those master lists too. Here and there the same middle-aged men would turn up, badly shaven, smelling of cologne, impatient and wary, but always polite. "How you doing, Father?" they'd ask.

But then one day, on a street even more narrow and tattered than most, its sidewalk broken and dog-fouled, we came upon

Abramson's little market. This one wasn't on the corner but half-way up the block. Neither the tough white boys nor their pudgy Catholic managers were loitering about. It was clear at first glance that this shop had been here a long while—much longer than the others we'd visited. Its shelves, stained now and dusty, had been solidly fashioned long ago out of wood, metal, thick strips of linoleum—whatever had come to hand. I wouldn't care to guess how long some of the cans and jars had stood undisturbed on those shelves.

The stock wasn't all that different from what we'd seen in the other small markets, though across from the gerbers and similac that the youth group kids were cataloguing there perched a shelf of dusty memorial candles and a few dwindling jars of matzo balls and gefilte fish. Behind the cash register an old man, Mr. Abramson as it turned out, was teasing into one of the jars with his thumb and forefinger, popping ragged bits of gefilte fish into his mouth. He watched us all the while, his eyes red-rimmed raw, his nose red too and cocked furiously in the air as he chewed.

It was me he was watching, though from the corner of his eye, darting it away when I glanced back at him. I'd guessed pretty quickly that the kids knew him. For the first time in all these weeks they were acting guilty rather than self-important as they tracked down the clipboard list, marking prices and supplies of baby formula. The Geiger twins stood at a metal rack of comic books, spinning it and studying Spiderman and ignoring the rest of us entirely. When the others had nearly finished, Abramson wiped his hands on a ratty towel and slipped out from behind the register.

"What're you doing?" he asked Michael, wedging in between us.

The boy froze, an awkward grin of nonchalance on his face. He looked young and naughty, caught elbow-deep in mischief.

"It's just a survey of baby supplies," I said to Abramson's back. From time to time on our other stops I'd begun to recite this same litany as a matter of form. The youth group was intent on community service, and the task was indeed worthwhile, and never before in that entire month had the words sounded so stiff, so absurd in my own ears.

Abramson paused one long moment to take it in. "I have been here a long time—I never do nothing to hurt babies," he said to Michael, puzzled and defensive. Then, angry at last, he straightened his back and turned towards me. The effort made him seem even older than I'd been guessing. His eyebrows were wild and furious. "What's wrong with my baby food? Is this what you really want?"

"*You, Priest.* What you want?" came a cry from the door. Pulling herself up the last step, a Black woman appeared, her bright purple dress stretched taut beneath a little jacket that hung open despite the cold morning. She swung into the market on her bad hip and cane, an empty plastic shopping-bag brandished in her other hand as she headed towards me. Where Abramson had spoken only to the kids, she addressed only me. "You doin' business here?" she asked, suddenly purring sweet, still panting from her rush up the steps.

I glanced at Michael, Mary, and Loretta, the three oldest members of the youth group, who were sidling farther down the aisle. Michael and Mary looked glum. Loretta's blue eyes brimmed with tears.

"Baby food," said Abramson, suddenly innocent as all the world. But he smiled, and I caught something sly and happy in his eye.

"Baby food?" Madelyn snorted. "Don't he know the little girls here feed they brats from the teat or with sugar water? They ain't smart enough to know to use your baby food."

Now she wheeled on me. (I nearly ducked). "And the boys who knocks up these little girls? They come right here three times last month. Got old Abramson to contribute to charity. Now you tell me, Priest—why don't they buy baby food with that money? Huh? *Baby food!*"

I wouldn't have blushed if the Geiger twins hadn't started giggling again.

"You Joshua," the woman yelled to the door. A man half her size, gnarled and dark as the tobacco twist he was stuffing quickly into his pocket, poked one foot in. "Spit that outer your mouth now—you got to give the priest and his children a ride home in this cold." Oh, she grinned, Joshua grinned, Abramson sagged, the twins giggled, my face was hot.

So Joshua wedged seven of us into his Oldsmobile for the eight block ride back to St. Stephen's. "She give it to you pretty good?" Joshua chuckled when we were safely away from the curb. "That's okay—my Madelyn does ev'ybody pretty good when she want to." A fresh chaw of tobacco swelled his cheek. He kept the window open far enough to spit.

Three weeks or so later, I returned the favor by dropping Madelyn on the corner of Abramson's market on my way downtown to fetch the old man out of jail. I tried to imagine him taking a shot at one of the neighborhood boys, and wondered how anyone could be so stupid. What kind of real trouble did he want?

Bail turned out to be a formality. They'd drop charges against Abramson in a day or two, the lieutenant explained while I waited for the paperwork to go through and for the prisoner to be released. The boy, Jamie, certainly wouldn't let himself be found, and no one else in the neighborhood was going to testify. The police had brought Abramson in only because he was still waving his pistol—registered and nearly obsolete—when they arrived at the market. They figured he needed a chance to calm down, while some of Jamie's friends could use the few hours without temptation for revenge or a little more play.

The lock on the steel door buzzed angrily and Abramson emerged with a stumble forward onto my arm. Quick as I could,

I sat him down on a wooden bench. Other visitors milled through and around us, some sitting on benches while grabbing hold of their childrens' arms or collars. Others rocked on their feet or huddled on the floor. And from the walls as much as from these visitors came the dull stink of stale sweat and beer and urine. Abramson was trembling, drawn into himself yet clutching my sleeve with one hand, unconscious of me as of a tree limb. His own arm felt brittle, lost in the folds of a frayed overcoat that had probably once fit him.

"I shot a boy," he murmured towards me. But I don't think he recognized Father Libberdi much beyond a vague notion that sometime or other I'd been in his market.

"He's okay," I said. "You missed."

"I shot one of those boys," he repeated, enough color to his voice this time that I realized the old man wasn't sorry so much as amazed, and not a little gleeful.

"You missed." I insisted on it.

But by slow degrees his face darkened as a new thought startled him. He seemed to withdraw farther into himself and the tattered coat. "An excuse," he murmured. "Oh, me—I am so stupid, I do not think." Pausing, he glanced sharply to one side and then the other, but not at me. I was still that tree limb, there only at the margin of his hand and his needs. His eyes were fever bright as he trembled.

"This is their excuse—they have waited for this. An excuse they always wait for. Then they come after us." He was panting. "Those boys, those boys. I let them take what they want—I must let them take what they want. But now they will come after us like they used to because I am such a fool."

Mr. Abramson was very far just then from Father Libberdi and the police station. Yet his fears and day-dreams, his confusion of one menacing world with another, irritated me as if chafing a sore I hadn't known was there and couldn't quite locate. My collar felt hot and tight.

Suddenly he was staring at me angrily, demandingly. "So, I have shot one of their boys." Still a defiant glee; still more a fresh anger. Abramson trembled.

"But you *missed*. No one's coming after you," I whispered furiously. I was uneasy, eager to get us away. "Your friend Madelyn sent me with the bail—nothing's changed." I gripped his shoulder in return, shaking him ever so lightly to make him listen.

Again he glanced at me, but in that single moment his eyes had dulled, their luster gone. "Please," he said softly, "take me home. I am very tired."

When we drove up to the market, Madelyn's Joshua was sitting vigil on the front steps. "Bring him on up," he called. "I got to put the old gangster to bed."

Even though I nearly carried him up the stone steps, Abramson was puffing hard by the time we got him into the shop. He lifted a hand to halt the procession before climbing the narrow stairs in back to his bedroom. "Close that door—lock it tight," he murmured to Joshua, arm round his neck. "They have their excuse now."

※

The woman tapped with her cane on the open door of my study. "Let me guess—he's in trouble again," I said. I'd been standing by the desk about to button on my collar and head off on a round of hospital visits. But a dull, oppressive sense of repetition, a sudden image of Madelyn enlisting me time and again to the end of time as a nursemaid for her Mr. Abramson, made my hand fall wearily away. I dropped the collar on the table.

This was maybe ten days since I'd seen her last. She looked weary herself, older than I remembered, perhaps even a bit frail despite her considerable size. The creases in her dark face were cut dry and deep. Not to say she didn't look petulant too.

"No—he ain't in trouble. Not the same way at least," she said with a sigh. She shuffled forward to my favorite reading chair and, loosening her short jacket, settled down heavily into it, her feet out. I swept up my collar again and swung away from the bare expanse of thigh where the woman's dress had ridden up.

"It's his sabbath tomorrow," she said. "And he wants to pray--say they comin' to get us and we got to be ready." With another sigh of exasperation she tugged the hem of her dress back down. "Lord knows he's right. Them boys gonna come back and keep comin' long as he keeps that shop open. I sure can't stop 'em on my own." She looked at me now as if somehow I were responsible for his stubbornness.

"You know, he don't need that shop no more. He's got money to get by, and him eighty-four years old already. Run from 'em once when he was a boy, he says, so he won't run this time. As if them boys care what he done before they own folks was born." Her voice slowly drifted away towards silence. Madelyn closed her eyes.

My part in the story, the heart of it, you see, lay in that moment, the old woman sprawled there in my study, nearly asleep, her feet splayed before her. For I realized then that the vague uneasiness I'd been feeling all along since her first visit was actually resentment. Resentment deep and heartfelt. I surely resented Madelyn's assumption that because my youth group and I had once transgressed by daring to question Abramson's supply of baby food, I had now to participate in her campaign for the health and safety of one old Jew.

Ah, but that's the easy side of it, such resentment is. All part of a priest's duty. Nothing more easily accepted and borne. This sudden crystallization of what had been a vague discontent into a declared foe made the issue all the more clear cut. That I'd do whatever Madelyn had come to ask was settled as automatically as I now picked up the collar from the desk once more and buttoned it on.

Yet, truth to tell, even as I was buttoning I realized that the teeth of the resentment dug a great deal deeper than that. Deeper than any immediate issue of Abramson's latest troubles or how glad I might be to help.

There aren't any other Jews for them to come after, there's only you, I'd wanted to shout at him in the police station as I shook him by the arm. *Your people left here long ago—there's only you. It's not because you're a Jew the boys come. Only because you're an old man with a little bit of money who's stayed past his time.*

Stubborn, sly, not entirely helpless, the old man might just as easily have clutched at my arm and whispered, *Priest, your people are leaving now—most of them gone already—what can you do for those who stay? I chose to stay. So you? Your bishop or whatever sends you here. Did you choose to come—do you choose to stay?*

As it was, I'd only shaken Mr. Abramson gently and said nothing. He said he was tired and wanted to go home. And in my own study ten days later, with Madelyn silent before me, I realized how deeply I resented what the old man might have said.

"He got to have a *min*-yon for his service," Madelyn said at last without stirring. "Ten men. Us gals don't count, naturally."

"He needs ten Jews," I said.

"So where you gonna find ten Jews around here? You gonna bus 'em all the way from Southfield like they was school kids? No suh, Mr. Priest. You and my others will do fine. If we gettin' ready for the end to come, you ten are good as any."

An hour before sundown that next day the sky darkened with clouds and a marrow-numbing cold whipped off the river. Yet rather than wrestle with the ancient Chrysler again, I hiked the eight blocks to Abramson's corner market.

As I climbed the front steps, I spotted two of my parishoners among six or seven women, black and white, clustered around the front counter. Madelyn herself was just then carrying two pink dinner candles up the narrow flight of stairs in back, shielding them as best she could from the blast of wind I'd let in. (I decided to leave the pair of candles I'd smuggled out of the vestry in my coat pocket).

"You come on up," she called back to me.

I hurried along behind her up the stairs and through a doorway. Waggling the candles dangerously in one hand, Madelyn wedged herself through the ten men or more who were already gathered in the small, stale room, and with her other hand set two small plates on a folding stand by the window. Dripping some wax onto the plates, she stuck the candles upright before hurrying out of the room.

Joshua was there, draped in a tattered prayer shawl, a small chaw of tobacco in his cheek. He glanced at me once and then away, an embarrassed grin on his face, refusing to meet my eyes.

Michael, from the youth group, stood off to one side and waved to me. He wore one of his father's caps—everyone had a hat— including his father, Joseph Trgovic, red-faced and heavy hammed, his baseball cap with a patch from a local brewery pushed back on his head. Trgovic saw me, pretended not to, stamped, shuffled as if cold, scowled, and screwed himself up all attention to Abramson.

The old man noticed none of this but inclined closer to the candles. He stood next to the window, bowed slightly as if the wind were pressing at him through the sooty glass. He was wearing the only other prayer shawl and a fedora that must once have been carefully brushed but was now a shiny greenish black. It rode on his ears. He was holding a ragged prayerbook close to the candles and peering into the reflected light from the page.

The whole of the cold journey from the vestry I'd been swearing (mildly) into the teeth of the wind that this was going to be pleasant. Community spirit after all. Different people come together in a common effort, sharing an experience long to be recalled as special, meaningful.

All we shared, as it turned out, was an embarrassed awkwardness. We could only stand and watch as Abramson fumbled his way through the prayer book, flipping back and forth and mumbling stray snatches of Hebrew that none of us, not a one, recognized. For that matter, the prayers didn't seem all that familiar to him either. Some came easier than the rest—what he remembered from boyhood no doubt. Even so, Abramson seemed oblivious to the rest of us, unconcerned that we couldn't participate with him.

Why did he want us here? I wondered. Were Blacks, Poles, Italians all Jews so long as they helped look after him? Or didn't even that matter—were we here not to participate after all, but simply to bear witness as he readied himself for what might come?

The old man's skin was as nearly the color of parchment as the leaves he turned, his lips colorless and dry save for a single bubble of spit, his eyes loosely shuttered as a dreamer's. Still, he seemed to me to be wearing that sly, subtle smile that gave nothing away. The deep resentment that was directed not so much at him as at myself flared again. I wished the whole thing would end quickly so I could get away and breathe.

Suddenly, without any warning at all, Abramson caught himself up short and glanced about the crowded room with a puzzled frown, as if he'd forgotten something he couldn't go on without. He rested his book by the candles and hurried across the hall into his bedroom.

Joshua tugged out a rag and spat his tobacco into it. "Ain't nothing we can do long's he keeps the shop," he said as if we knew it already. "If they *do* come and get him, again and again, they ain't nothing we can do." He spat reflectively once more into the rag and tucked it back in his coat pocket.

So sharing something now after all—our helplessness to protect this stubborn old man—we waited silently in the dusk of the candles for him to return.

The moment dragged on. Someone coughed. I smiled at Michael. We were restless and the stirring made the room seem more crowded. At last Joshua slipped out and across the hall. Something about his haste had me darting after him, the others crowding behind me into the bedroom.

The first thing Joshua did was flip on a hanging bulb. There lay Abramson on a broken-backed couch across from the narrow cot, his head to one side, the fedora fallen awry on the floor. He was napping. In his hands he clutched a half-empty bottle of purple wine. He must have come to fetch it for a blessing and sat on the couch—only for a moment of course (maybe he'd sipped the wine too)—but he'd dozed before remembering to rise again.

He was smiling now like a sleepy child, nothing sly to him, as Joseph Trgovic picked him up gently and eased him onto the bed. Abramson stirred a little. "My shoes," he said, draping his legs over the side for me to unknot the laces and pull the shoes off.

When I came downstairs the others were already passing a pint of whiskey. They were silent and serious about it, chagrined only when I appeared. One of the women tucked it hastily into her coat.

"I might try a taste of that," I said.

She brought it forth again hesitantly. Joseph Trgovic rooted up a plastic cup from behind the counter and handed it to Michael for me, as if being dainty might mitigate the deed. But I stuck the bottle to my mouth and swallowed once, twice, before the taste could stop me cold. It was corn whiskey and raw and I choked, my eyes tearing, and that seemed to make it better for the rest of them. Someone chuckled—probably Joshua again. I took another tentative sip and passed the whiskey on.

That smoothed over the rest of it, the drink did. Not that there was enough whiskey to make much difference, except to make the roots of my teeth ache. Yet, after all, we'd completed in a rough sort of way the ceremony for which Abramson had gone to fetch the wine.

PLAY

The day James Russell returned to Meadowbrook School after nine months of attending another junior-high downtown—closer to his mother's family—he discovered a set of initials, SAP, painted crudely on the school's neat white brick entrance. Then, there again, only a few yards away, SAP bled scarlet through a fresh coat of white paint. As James wandered through the halls that day he spotted the same letters carved into desk tops, burned with matches into toilet stalls, streaked with marker across windows in the library.

At another school these might have been a special girl's initials or a gang's acronym. But such things were new to this small town, suddenly discovering itself to be one of the older suburbs and apparently closer to the city than it had been aware. S.A.P. were only the initials of a twelve year old mulatto boy, small for twelve, whose skin was more a jaundiced orange than either white or black.

Late in the afternoon that first day back, James Russell took a seat by the windows before fifth-period math class. While he and the others waited for their teacher, Stevie Peters tumbled into the classroom, his nose running, his shirt buttoned askew, wrong hole to wrong button, half its tail tucked into the stretchband of his underwear. Taunts flared from around the room with brutal exhilaration. James Russell jerked his head up. "Sap," they were calling, whining at Stevie. "Sap—you so gross, boy. You, Sap." Blacks jeered and whistled from the back of the room. Whites jeered and whistled and cried from their greater territory. Stevie hesitated, dazed but not surprised. He wiped at his nose with a shirt sleeve, smearing his face hopelessly. For a single long moment he hung there at the front of the room, grinning and foolish, and then paper flew, and a book, another, and Stevie ducked, scurrying for his seat just as Mr. Andrews appeared in the door.

James Russell never stirred. From his desk to one side he watched, his face smooth, very black. His eyes did narrow a bit, a certain sort of look he'd had since he was a little boy, detached and skeptical, puzzled and intent. He wore it while stalking through each step of a math puzzle; had worn it defensively (it finally set like lock-jaw) these past nine months downtown in the face of his grandmother's Pentecostal passion, until Mama finally found her new job with a white family up this way.

And here was Stevie—oh, yes, he knew Stevie—standing and grinning for them, for the white boys and black boys, their jeers and their missiles, before fleeing to his desk. *You're the one. Gotta be*, James thought, blinking his eyes rapidly a few times as if to flick Stevie Peters away. A surge of shame and disgust tightened his throat.

Back before Mama lost her job and she and James had to move downtown, Stevie's mother had died and, only a couple months later, James' father disappeared. So the father and the mother who remained became friends—sometimes more—and their sons were brought to play together.

Together in a room or one corner of the weed-and-concrete playground, but not really *with* each other. Inside, with his math puzzles, his geometry, James discovered parts and bound them together. With the stuff of the world, however, he studied the lovely parts of what had been flawed, fragile wholes. He'd make something of nothing by pulling it apart, tearing and twisting piece from piece—a blade of crabgrass, an old clock from a bin. Even his hands and fingers he'd study with that narrow-eyed look from very far away, smiling at his command and their response. But if the fingers failed him, stumbling in their own innocence across shoelaces or slicing themselves bloody on a metal edge, his dark face grew darker still with an eight-year-old's vexation. And all the while he'd never make a sound.

Stevie shied away when that look came over James' face, though he might have been back home for all the look included him. He swung his feet around the other way in the dust. Warm at first touch, the dust quickly cooled as it clung to his orange skin, darkening him so that he might almost be James' shadow. It climbed and swam over his calves, up into his shorts, in smears across his face, as he scratched the earth before him with a stick.

James glanced at the other boy's dirty back, at the way he cocked his head while drawing. *I don't like you*, he wanted to say so bad he couldn't swallow all the spit.

But in the dirt Stevie was scratching magic with his twig. Quick strokes and a tree. Stick figure of a man—no, but no dead stick—this full of breath and speed. No one in school could do that, not even Miss Roberts with her smock and her water colors.

James watched from the corner of his eye so Stevie wouldn't notice. Those drawings made his own fingers feel plenty clumsy. But he did love the magic drawings even so, (he'd catch his own breath as if the sticks were about to fly away free), though he'd no love for the boy who sketched them. With a giggle and sigh, Stevie swiped his hand through the dust, scattering the figures into a cloud, and turned his grimy face to discover where James wanted to go next.

※

After the bell rang, Silas Andrews set his chalk aside and waited for the classroom to clear. In the loosed din of laughter and chatter, his white students surged first to the door, girls slipping ahead out to the sidewalks, while the blacks lingered behind sniggering and watching for the way to open.

A couple of trailing white boys coaxed Stevie Peters roughly out of his chair. They heaved him up by the arms, laughed, thumped his back to show Mr. Andrews that this was all in fun. Stevie hung back on his heels, grimacing but silent. As they dragged the boy along, ten or twelve black students streamed round them towards the door—a couple three slipped up on Stevie from behind and shoved him forward, grinning and dancing and hissing *Sap* in his ears.

Impassive, Andrews crossed his hands on the desk. Turning his head and staring out the window, he appeared deliberately unaware of what the boys were up to. In fact, he waited only for the first whimper of protest from Stevie Peters. Despite the noise from everyone else, he'd hear. But they sucked Stevie right on through the door and Silas Andrews might almost have shrugged as he settled back in his chair.

For the most part his students, white or black, kept to themselves. There'd been no open warfare, though Andrews foresaw it might yet come to that. Indeed, there were times he felt he was witnessing an inexorable disintegration of the school he'd taught in for twenty-three years, as if charting the course of disease in an old friend who no longer recognized him.

The white students hardly claimed his loyalty—their appalachian-hick families were as much intruders as the blacks'. Older families from this town had drifted away, or the sons and daughters of former students were enrolled in newer schools a couple miles north. White and black, the newcomers faced each other down—so far without open violence--and shared the tormenting of the mulatto boy.

Silas Andrews was a tall, gaunt man. His wild shock of ivory hair seemed always an odd contradiction to a meticulously trimmed, iron-grey moustache and to jaunty clothes ten years or more out of fashion. According to ancient habit, Andrews remained at his desk for half an hour after the final class on Tuesdays and Thursdays. But few students lingered anymore for help with homework or extra tutoring. Recently he'd taken to skipping out himself after the room emptied, rather than see the time through. For by late afternoon his ankles and calves ached, and the enormous claw-footed bath at home seemed the loveliest thing in the world.

Today, however, even before the last of the others had gathered their books and fled to the corridors, he sensed one boy waiting behind expectantly. At first Silas Andrews, surprised more than really pleased, didn't recognize him. The better part of a year had passed since the then seventh-grader had loitered in the hall until he could slip past older students hurrying the other way and take his place at that same desk. "I see you're back with us, Mr. Russell," said Andrews matter-of-factly after a long moment. Tugging a wrinkled handkerchief from his jacket, he wiped his hands.

"I'd like to work some more math," said James.

"Naturally," Andrews murmured. He drew two loose sheets of paper from a notebook he'd been ready to close. Rising stiffly, bursitis raw in his hip, he placed the frayed and rather dirty pages on the desk in front of James. These extra problems, diagrams, and explanations belonged to a stillborn textbook Andrews had composed fifteen years before. The boy nodded and immediately bent forward, pencil gripped knuckle tight. His teacher paused, wiping his hands again, and observed the first exercise.

The boy rocked unconsciously back and forth in his seat like some old Jew Andrews had once seen praying. Shoulders and head rocked a few inches, gentle, steady. The sleeves of his not-quite-threadbare blue shirt had been cut short and neatly hemmed, probably because its elbows defied further patching. But it was the boy's face Andrews found himself staring at from an oblique angle. An impassive ebony mask neither young nor old, innocent of passion in its detached concentration, its gentle rocking, masking even whether the boy enjoyed this extra study.

Blowing his nose into the handkerchief once and for all broke the spell and Andrews returned to his desk. And he realized with a grim sort of satisfaction that he resented the boy. Here he was, appearing out of nowhere and demanding attention. What right had he?

Silas Andrews had withdrawn further and further into routine these last few years. Sheltered there, he watched for the approaching floodtide. He'd an urgency to witness what was to come, to taste the worst, yet not be swept up and away. And so far routine had indeed protected him. His students did the work they were prepared to do. If they didn't bother to obey him, they let Andrews be. Behavior, in fact, was less a problem in his classes than in some where teachers crowed or bullied or pleaded for what they took to be respect. His students laughed at Andrews' two-tone shoes, at his high-waisted trousers and neatly pressed suits. They laughed and humored him like an exotic bird they'd adopted as pet.

So this boy, this James Russell, perched at his desk, neither sullen nor aloof, simply absorbed in the delicate flowering of geometric proofs. And guilty though he surely felt, Andrews resented him.

He realized he'd been staring again only when James glanced up and their eyes met. The boy's were alight—sharp and clear and intoxicated all at once. His lips parted slightly. Feeling suddenly confused and vulnerable, the old man dropped his gaze to the papers in his open briefcase, and his resentment swelled with blood in his ears.

"If you haven't finished yet, Mr. Russell, just take the rest of it along with your homework," he muttered. Embarrassed with his own impatience, Andrews kept his head tucked down all the while. His legs ached.

James blinked. For an instant he'd hardly been aware of Silas Andrews. But even before his teacher spoke, the look in his eyes, cornered and nasty, shivered into James. "No," he said, "I just got done." Slipping out from the desk, he presented the pages, the original two and one more covered with his own work, to his teacher. "Thank you," he said. It sounded stiff and hurt.

A dull anger had welled up in James Russell, as if the old white man's glance, dried up and cold, had stolen away something precious. As he gathered his books and left the classroom, he swore he wouldn't leave himself open to be robbed the next time.

Except for a pick-up basketball game off to one side, the schoolyard was deserted as James stood blinking into the harsh leafless glare of mid-autumn. Off to one side by the high fence Stevie Peters huddled over a chalk sketch he'd nearly finished on the asphalt. Not a yard beyond him another set of his own initials were spray-painted candy pink. James wandered to his side, hoping uneasily that the boys playing basketball wouldn't notice him talking to their SAP.

James clutched his books to his chest as Stevie stroked out the final limbs of a spare, two-masted ship. After the rigid necessity of geometry's lines and arcs, such freehand boldness of white chalk on dark pavement was as startling as the late-afternoon sun. Stevie drew his hand back and the ship soared on asphalt.

"You come a ways, boy," James said softly. "You never done nothing like that before."

"What d'you know? Where you been to see?" Stevie snapped. Caught off guard, James Russell said nothing.

Stevie hunkered back on his heels the way his daddy did. He never glanced up at the boy over his shoulder. The ship he stared at. Then kneeling forward again he circled it with a violent swoop of chalk. A diagonal slash cut through ship guts. Another blasted its masts into confusion. Again and again Stevie criss-crossed the circle until, in the chalk patch on the schoolyard, nothing of his ship remained.

James had held his ground. But his jaw was trim with anger when Stevie rose. "*Crazy,*" he said. "You shouldn't a."

Stevie grinned and cocked his head, leaned up close to James. "They gonna piss on it if I leave it—why should I leave it?" he whispered. Snuffling, he flipped away the chalk stub and set off trudging slowly towards the street.

Stevie Peters smelled funny—*smelled bad*—and that tight disgust climbed into James's throat again, so there wasn't even much room left anymore for anger.

✳

Nearly every morning Silas Andrews spent first light in his small rose garden, trousers and shirt sleeves turned up, his silk tie laid out in the kitchen next to a thermos he'd fill with hot tea before leaving for school. After a few moments as he dragged the trowel along, his hair abandoned its part and, above Silas' starched collar and brass-tipped suspenders, was once again as untamable a thatch as any boy could boast.

Late autumn gave him half-an-hour's light for turning soil and mulch. His hip and shoulders and calves loosened. And what the trowel stiffened in turn—especially his back—would stretch free enough to get him through the day during his walk to school.

Arriving as usual before anyone except the custodian, Andrews poured a first cup of tea. His shoulder-bag with books and papers and lessons he set by the leg of his desk and stood in the window with the mug he kept locked in a drawer. Although the school was nestled halfway down an easy slope towards a stream, Andrews' window faced up towards Meadowbrook Road. A couple of years ago its elms, which had come to reach across almost into each other's arms, had suddenly failed one after the other, as if the initial loss had weakened the survivors' resolve. Chain saws and sawdust and falling limbs heartened the town planners, who quickly scored a beastly yellow line down the center of the lane. Andrews sipped his tea and resented the nakedness of his window to passing cars.

Sometimes he had a distant sort of sympathy for those elms. Seeing what was to come, one humiliating failure after another, they'd gone and got out of it. The elms, the yellow strip, the initials S.A.P. first inked onto his blotter and then carved deeply into the desk top.

They hounded and tormented that boy, never quite injuring him. No, it was his sheer humiliation they were after, again and again. Out of it surged some shared exhilaration, and so there was no need to go after each other.

A couple of times in and around the school Andrews had caught them at it. They'd break off and leave him the boy, clothes ravaged, face smeared with ink or mud or his own snot. Andrews, as disgusted with Stevie as with his tormentors, sent him home to be cleaned up—there was nothing more he could do for him here.

✳

It didn't take long that fall for James to realize that Stevie was steering clear of him. After all, the little bungalow that Stevie and his father lived in was only a couple of blocks from James' and his mama's apartment. But Stevie darted straightaway from school every afternoon. He'd probably discovered a new retreat somewhere, a new patch of pavement for his sketches. So James walked home alone, though other kids bobbed and skittled all around him. They liked him well enough, he knew, but in a suspicious sort of way. They didn't know what to do when, from being just like any of them—listening to music from someone's radio, waving his arms and shoulders and head, if not quite dancing along—he'd suddenly draw back cold, his face impassive or slightly puzzled, a thousand miles distant. A girl had smiled or he'd imagined one smiling or the afternoon bus from the north end of town had swung by with his mother and the other maids, and then he wasn't with the other kids anymore but alone, watching himself walk home among them.

He tried not to see himself, even walked long yards of sidewalk with his eyes shut tight. But only the music was lost then, shut out—didn't sound like music anymore—and while the others danced on, he felt the clumsy jar of each heel striking, each stiff step of the way.

Nor did it take James long to discover that Mama's new job wasn't the only reason she'd borrowed family money so they could hurry back out of the city. He figured he should have known all along. For most every night Stevie's father, Byron Peters, arrived in time for the apple pie or fritters Mildred Russell had begun in the morning and finished before changing out of her maid's uniform late in the afternoon.

Byron Peters was a big light-skinned black man, good looking, a great bear of a friendly man, limping aggressively on a right foot whose toes he'd lost in Georgia between a tractor and a pine tree. After dessert he and Mildred sat on the little apartment's porch, whole evenings in silence and light from a single lamp. Byron never had much to say. He spoke with this big grin of his and with his hands. In an evening he might whittle a toy for Mildred from a small block of wood or see to little jobs around her apartment. Tiny Mildred, hardly taller than Byron even while he kneeled in a clutter of pipes and wrenches and washers, stood just behind, reaching out from time to time, her cool hand testing the heat of his neck, jerking it back almost at touch, smiling.

James bolted his dessert, and Mama didn't even scold him. She used to make these special treats for him. The two of them might spend an hour nipping at her blackberry pie and ice cream, and laughing, teasing the sweetness along. Now, once he'd scraped his bowl clean, James disappeared into his room with homework or wandered out along the street.

Stevie was avoiding him. They'd be brothers if it happened—he'd think it, clenching his teeth. The cry he'd strangle back so only he heard. He didn't want Stevie—he wanted Mama—but Byron Peters was gonna have Mama, and he'd get Stevie. A brother. But he didn't like him—he smelled bad. James was relieved not to have Stevie follow him around the way he used to, so the others could see.

The night was cool, blanched with moon and pockets of street lamps. No stars and no Stevie. James wore two shirts and a t-shirt underneath, hiking along quick enough so what he wore was enough. Had he done something to drive the orange-skinned boy away? Though he couldn't think of anything, he felt guilty—he might have done it, had wanted to.

Down behind the all-night party store two boys—a couple year older than him—had got someone to buy them a bottle of wine. They swilled it back so their mouths couldn't catch it all. Down their chins the red wine trickled and blotched their shirts. Spotting James they waved the bottle in its brown bag and giggled.

"Wannah?" they called.

"Nah," he said with a toss of his hand, and felt lonelier still.

※

By mid-November there were other students, three and four and six at a time—and not always the same ones—staying late on Tuesdays and Thursdays for extra tutoring. Perhaps because the November weather hardly invited them out to play. Perhaps because they'd seen James Russell be so regular about doing the same thing week after week.

Startled, certainly, by this flurry of attention, and tickled by the amazement of his younger colleagues, Silas Andrews was, nevertheless, not at all persuaded that he wouldn't prefer it all to die away and leave him in peace once more. He'd reach home at the end of the day with aching legs and empty thermos, and all the day's light—what there was of it in November—had been snatched away by wind and the low scud of clouds. He'd even taken to leaving on a small porcelain lamp inside the cottage door just to greet him home.

Now, truth was, (though Andrews didn't say it to himself in so many words), he hadn't really expected James Russell to turn up again after their first session at the beginning of the term. Silent as they'd been, they'd both been angry—he'd expected an end to it. Yet come Tuesday, and then again Thursday here the boy remained, his place off to one side by the windows.

Andrews remembered what they used to call them when they were dark as that—a purple nigger, they'd call him.

Embarrassed at the tone of his own father's voice so many years ago and at the way a dab of spittle might catch in the corner of the old man's mouth when said and done, Andrews snatched the handkerchief from his breastpocket and blew his nose. Two of the students who'd stayed behind today glanced up. Not James Russell. No, there was no denying, Andrews admitted, the boy was dark as night and sullen beyond words and he wouldn't so much as acknowledge his teacher anymore. Even when accepting the day's assignment and then laying the completed sheets on the front desk, the boy cocked his head away.

Hot with elation, James slipped the papers onto his teacher's desk. "Thank you," he said to the desk, never lifting his eyes. No one was going to steal anything from him again. He saw Andrews' hand draw the pages in, but the old man said nothing, and James clutched his books and headed out of the room.

Shouts cannoned out from behind the closed door of a bathroom in the corridor, laughter ricocheting off tiles. As James Russell approached he could make out, underneath the harsh preying cries, a soft blubbering broken only by gulps for air. James heard a deep thud and slap of skin on skin, a low moan, and then the blubbering caught its track once more.

Dropping his books on a window ledge, he stared at the bathroom door, knowing he had to look and not wanting to. And when he pushed on through and saw, he stopped short again, disgust and anger and misery tight in his throat. A couple of the boys glanced back at him; the others didn't bother. At their feet whimpered Stevie—dirty, orange, fleshy, his pants tangled at his knees. They'd torn him out of a stall. A black boy slashed a red crayon at his face and belly, while one of the white boys held a notebook with Stevie's crayon sketch exposed. Lifting it daintily by a corner, he leaned over the lump of flesh on the floor and swung the notebook out through the air. Wings of paper flapped as it tumbled towards the toilet.

"Stop it," James cried.

"Yo, Sap—hah!" they cried, heads lifted, nostrils flared. The walls drummed back their shouts. They heard nothing, saw no one—not each other's color—only the thing that had wet itself and the tiles it huddled on.

Andrews and the two white students who'd remained in the classroom looked up as the door jerked open. His chest heaving, James Russell beckoned the teacher. "Please," he said. "You gotta come."

Andrews grunted, heaved himself up, and followed the boy who'd already fled before him. The other two, Sarah Marshall and Tim Rainy, crowded him along from behind. Too fast, too fast. He wanted dreadfully to see, but he was scared. Which of the nightmares he'd foreseen for his school had arrived?

"Hurry, hurry," urged the two behind him. They could already hear the tumult.

James Russell had wheeled ahead of them in the hall, waiting without speaking again, but glaring, his eyes white hot and demanding. Those eyes seemed to mock Andrews for his slowness, his age, his fear. Silas Andrews hated James Russell.

"Stop that whining, you gross meat," rang through the air. "Make him—gonna make him stop."

The boy shoved the bathroom door open and paused on its threshold, one foot in. Andrews peered past him but went no further. Amidst their whoops and hollers, the five boys driving Stevie back into his stall heard nothing behind them. They kicked and shoved and nudged him, though with an awkward sort of gentleness—their kicks missed entirely or glanced off his naked buttocks.

"You missed him again—how you miss something that fat?"

"Too gross for me—why I wanna touch something that gross?"

Andrews saw James Russell, standing in the door, struggle, the ebony mask stretched taut, anguished, no longer impassive, its lines too rigid, eyes too bright. The boy glared at the old man, ferocious and despairing.

"You gonna *do* something?—You gonna stop 'em?" he demanded.

Andrews hated James Russell. The hair on his brow felt damp, worrisome as an insect. He brushed it back with his hand. His legs trembled—but they'd do that sometimes this late in the day.

"They're playing," he mumbled, and knew he was grinning stupidly, grotesquely.

"*What* d'you say?" James roared hoarsely and let the door swing to. The bathroom flashed quiet. Even the blubbering caught its breath.

"They're playing," Andrews repeated more loudly. "No one's being hurt. It's a game they're all playing." He paused, pursing his lips, and then he went on more softly, triumphant and not a little vicious. "Why should I want to stop them, Mr. Russell? So they can go out and fight in the street? You *want* that? You want to stop it? Tell them the custodian will be locking up soon. It's time to go home."

Light-limbed and giddy, Silas Andrews strolled down the hall to his classroom, not once looking back. Sarah and Tim glanced at the bathroom door, glanced at James, and giggled nervously, their heads bent together, before racing after their teacher to retrieve their own books.

James Russell stood alone in the hall.

After another long moment the bathroom door cracked, swung full open. One after another five boys, eighth and ninth graders, slipped out. They grinned at each other. The last of them, Sammy, tall, lean, and brown, toothpick swaggered in his lips, stopped next to James and grinned. "You some real shit be doin' that to us, brother," he hissed softly, and trotted away after the others.

Numb, James hesitated a while longer before heading once more into the bathroom. Stevie Peters had tugged up his soiled pants, but he still sat on the floor. He was snuffling and breathing hard through his mouth. One of his socks lay close by in a puddle.

"You *want* something?" he whined harshly.

"Nah," said James. The boy's naked foot stuck out pale as the belly of a dead fish. "Want some help?" he asked. With his foot he nudged the sock out onto a dry tile.

"I don't want *nothing*."

James' eyes darted to Stevie again, startled at the fury in his voice.

"Why cain't you let it alone? I don't want your help—nothing from you so high and clean. You and your mama got my daddy all right. But you alone, boy—got no friends like me." He waved his hand in the air after the friends who'd just disappeared. Tears were flowing now, a gentle stream down his face he couldn't blink away. "You mind your own damn business."

Anger gone, heat all spent, James figured he should be crying too, but the only feeling left him was a cold-fisted knot in his belly. *My mama and your daddy, and you gonna be my brother,* he thought. The thought was cold and empty as all the rest, unreal. He shrugged and turned away.

Out in the schoolyard, dusk settled cool and rich and full. No one was about. James dropped his books and pulled a sweatshirt on over his head. And he sat right down on the asphalt, chin on fists. He wished something would happen, that he'd start trembling or crying or that the sky would fall. Dusk deepened towards night.

The old man was right, and James snorted at the thought. They were playing. It was playing because Stevie played along too, did what the rules gave him to do. Suddenly another thought dropped over him like a net out of the night sky. *Stevie must want it, all the attention.* James Russell shook his head, shook back and forth so that his whole body rocked on the pavement. All the rest, anger and surprise and nausea all shook free into the twilight before this one surprise for which he had no answer. Stevie was playing along with those friends of his.

Instead of heading home directly when he rose at last, James wandered down to the small brook behind the school. The little bit of water sluiced its way along. No birds, hardly a breeze, the only sound rose from a faint rush of water among pebbles. Bright lights from the school parking lot fleshed out the darkness down here below.

Without sitting on the bank, he carefully removed his shoes and socks, rolled his pants up, and waded out into the brook. The water reached only to his ankles. It was very cold. Stones were sharp and smooth and treacherous. He smiled because no one could see. So Stevie played. And Mr. Andrews allowed the play—did that mean he took his own part in the game?

As his toes numbed to the water James halted in midstream so he wouldn't stumble, but he didn't climb out. Could he go home for supper and find nothing changed? Stevie's father come for dessert, homework to finish?

His toes were quite numb. His feet ached. That he didn't feel lonely was the only surprise left him. Weary, yes, and his feet did ache—but no loneliness anymore—he'd been stripped clean of it and could breathe.

Alone and not lonely, James Russell stumbled up out of the brook, pulled his socks and shoes on, though he had to sit down to do it, and, toes stinging enough nearly to blind him, set off home for his supper.

WHEN THE TIME IS RIGHT

For two-and-a-half years, Saul and I went to Kingsmount's chapel with everyone else. He'd decided almost from the beginning that there wasn't anything wrong with the Lord's Prayer; he'd even practice reciting it under his breath as we walked back to our dorm on Sunday mornings. By the winter of our third year, I felt irked and not a little puzzled. Why was he the one so comfortable with it?

"What the hell are you doing, saying that all the time?" I finally demanded. It was Sunday and cold. We were hiking back half a mile through the snow, and I'd just stepped through a film of ice into an ankle-deep puddle. I limped along, shaking my foot every few steps and cursing as the water soaked through my sock. Saul looked at me as if I were crazy. Dismayed, embarrassed, he didn't say anything as we followed the road, but he glanced down at my wet shoe as if it were to blame.

He sounded cocky when we went to see the headmaster two days later. We marched into the dark, paneled office at the designated hour, he first and I on his heels.

"Sir, Teddy and I don't want to go to chapel here anymore."

I winced. He was brash and sounded it, and I couldn't say a mitigating word.

"And why is that?" Mr. Fielding looked startled.

The son of a bitch cocked his head and smiled innocently. "He's Irish, sir, and I'm a Jew. We want to go into town for that sort of thing."

The thick gray eyebrows shrugged high on old Fielding's brow as he nodded, weighing it. "Yes," he said, "I think we can manage something. Arrange it, then clear the plans with me, Mr. Shannon," he declared, addressing me. He was pleased with himself just then, I think—as pleased as Saul was with himself.

"I'm not Irish. My great-grandfather was Irish," I hissed, as we went through the outer office.

"With that name, you'll always be Irish, or I'm no Jew," he said, grinning. And, with a triumphant toss of his head, he strutted off to the library. On weekends thereafter, we went up to Winketauk together, one Sunday to the Catholic church and the next Saturday to the tiny synagogue. At first it was difficult. I didn't much like wearing the little cap or listening through the prayerbook Hebrew, but at least there was an English version on the facing page. Saul in his turn wasn't thrilled about being left alone while I went up for communion, but he did like all the Latin. After a while, we both began to enjoy the quiet and peace of those mornings—so much so that we rarely used them, as we easily might have, to sneak out to Lake Ontario or simply to wander through the town.

That year, when we were in third form, we joined one of the school's football teams. Six months older, an inch taller, stronger if a shade slower, I was a better player than Saul. Almost every day after practice we'd stay on, just the two of us, throwing and catching the ball until we were blistered with mud, our fingers so numb in the wind whipping off Lake Ontario ten miles away that we could hardly hold the ball.

With classes and football, we were kept busy. I did pretty well, except for the Latin. Saul could do Latin, rattling off the cases—thank God, without smiling—hardly glancing at his book. To have him sit there reading while I struggled with Caesar got to be too much. Every fifteen seconds or so, I'd look up and call out a question which he'd answer without breaking mental stride. I wouldn't have minded if only it disturbed him.

Our team played four games that fall. Two were with the public school down the road, one on their field and one at Kingsmount. I didn't know there were as many kids in all of upstate New York as came for the first game. They had cheerleaders for their freshman team. We had thirteen players, including the kid who forgot his shoes and played in laced oxfords—and me, making my debut as quarterback.

Scared and nervous, yes, me with my hands up under the center's butt, and we managed to drop the ball on two of the first three snaps. When they kicked off after scoring, we fumbled on the second play. That was enough for our coach—the Latin master, as it happened—who ordered Saul and me to trade positions. So he debuted at quarterback that day too. After I'd taken his place as an end, the only time I touched the ball for the rest of the game was while we were on defense and a badly thrown pass plunged lamely into the mud at my feet.

Saul quarterbacked each of the next three games; we even managed to win one of them. I knew then that our Latin master, and the varsity coach himself, had seen a spark in him. They'd spotted something, his quickness most likely, or his confidence—and he remained at quarterback and I was an end and we never stayed late at practice again.

The next summer, before our sophomore year, Saul worked at his father's stamping plant in Cleveland. From seven in the morning until five, he bound sheets of steel together with razor-sharp bands, heaving up two-hundred-pound bundles with another boy onto flatbed trailers. The first thing he showed me in the fall was the long blue-white scar where a steel strip had whipped back and sliced through his thigh. He was proud of it—like a scar of honor, I imagined then—but it was more the covenant he'd made with himself, part of the price he was willing to pay.

With the strength from the job, he'd also gained weight, especially through his chest and shoulders: nearly two inches of height had come of their own accord. I'd been living with this guy for three years, but at football practice in August I was looking at a stranger. He'd grown past me in one fertile summer—he even looked taller than six feet. The way he carried himself, with those hazel eyes and the beaked nose, and the very fine dark hair, was striking. I was a little breathless with surprise at all the changes, not to say a bit scared.

The coach spared Saul and the number one quarterback the contact drills. They stood along the sidelines, rocking forward heel to toe, arching long passes to panting receivers. The ball soared forty and forty-five yards from Saul's hand, and I could see from the center of the field that he didn't even bother to grunt.

I was the fodder. As an underclassman I was the one they jammed the ball to, aimed at two linemen and ordered to run through them. So I did—that is, I ran at them, not through.

Not a few of us passed up dinner that night. After a long shower, I walked very slowly from the gym to our room, so slowly that the dust on the brick paths didn't puff beneath my feet. The August day was still very hot, and the sky, bleached and faded, rang with light. I lay down on my bed, naked except for my shorts, the soreness and aches gathering, settling in my ribs and the fleshy muscles along my thighs and crotch. I lay there like that for two hours without stirring, scarcely breathing, because even that hurt.

When Saul finally came into the room, the daylight had worn itself to dusk. The shadows weren't much cooler, but they were soothing. With the first stirring of an evening breeze, insects were humming outside. Neither of us spoke for a while. I heard him arranging something on his desk.

I don't know how long it was before he slapped me once at the base of my neck. I may have been dozing because suddenly, with the slap, the darkness was fleshed and secure.

"It'll be a long two weeks in Boston, Teddy." I hadn't said a word, but he guessed.

"Yeah," I muttered into the pillow.

For several moments we were silent. I could hear him breathing. Then his cool hand returned, touching me again, cool against my shoulder, turning me away from the pillow. It was rough and clumsy, and I didn't shove him away because he'd already pulled back. He stood in the middle of the floor and I could see his face, its hard, pale features, in the final benevolence of twilight or my own imagination. In another moment, he'd gone silently, leaving me to the night and peace and the insects' garrulous hum.

The kiss was a consummation of something that had never needed one before. I wasn't angry, I wasn't surprised—had the throw been mine, I'd have done the same, perhaps.

I skipped curfew that night. The estate around the school was quiet and deserted. A dirt path led me through the woods until it strayed across a shallow meadow. The stream which tossed off diagonally here wound its way back toward the campus.

I waded out, shoes on the bank, cuffs rolled up. The water came only to mid-calf, but it was cool and dark, brushing past me, and I cupped my hand and drank. A long while later, barefoot, I strolled back along the bank. Saul was asleep when I returned; in the morning, the sun dim with heat when I woke, he wasn't there.

I had this friend Michael, who was hot about the dramatic society—or, more particularly, about a local girl who helped with the costumes. In the middle of September, when he was going to the gym to audition for the next play, he suggested I take a shot at it. Under his arm he carried a book to read from and I dug out a soliloquy to try.

A week later, after shoving me down three steps and into a stand of garbage cans, Michael told me I'd been given the male lead. There's nothing more suspect than someone who's young and thinks he can act—and, since I hadn't started to yet, apparently the director thought I'd be safe.

Rehearsals were at night, so I could make it to the home football games. Our senior quarterback was good that year; he ran better than he threw, getting what he needed from the others, enough to eat up four or six yards at a crack. But, late in the season, he got hurt. He got to his feet, but didn't come back to the bench. He swayed along slowly with one of the coaches, past the visitors' bench, right arm tucked to his side. We all knew it was bad.

So Saul got his chance. In the game with Bay Point, second to the last, the final one at home, he was sent out to quarterback. I was proud of him, the way he trotted onto the field, not too quickly, confidently. He didn't look cocky from where I sat—but maybe the other players thought so, because they died. They might as well have quit playing then and there. Saul would spin to hand the ball off, and before the runner could so much as look for a hole everyone but the Bay Point coach and mascot had him buried.

Only the seniors, the sixth formers who'd be gone the next year, really mourned. The rest of us saw magic enough to wait for. That day Saul threw the ball only four times. He'd drop back five or six steps, his hand cocked at his ear, and they'd rush and tumble all over themselves to get him. They never did. He seemed always to know to the fraction of a second how long he had, and in that last pulse his wrist shot the ball clear, thirty-five or forty yards on a line. Not one of those passes was caught, as if the receivers were startled by the ball. But we all saw enough, and in the season's last game one of them did catch the ball for a long touchdown.

People are eager to adore. But for the untimely return of parents, I believe Saul would have lost the virginity I thought he still owned to one of three local girls who met the team bus after that last game in Pennsylvania. He escaped rather miraculously, it seemed to me, without owing embarrassment either to the girls or the parents, let alone the school.

Of course I envied him—but not as much as I might have. After all, we weren't competing for the same laurels anymore. And it was an exciting time, those nine months before, as a junior, he could quarterback the team. He wasn't a full-fledged hero yet, and those of us who knew him treasured what was to come. It's heady stuff, sharing that kind of secret—more potent than any future consummation because then we'd have to share. Memories aren't potent, unless they force you to tell.

He came to two of the four performances of our play, a dreadful little romance written by the drama coach in his college days, and on our way to church a week later he slapped my arm and swore he'd enjoyed it. That was all. But I'd done little more than clap him on the shoulder after his performance as a quarterback. We weren't slighting each other, but we were discovering how little we had to say. That night in August, which we'd neither forgotten nor regretted, had stolen our words.

Spring hadn't really arrived—it was the hopeful, tentative warmth of an early thaw, a false spring, that made an early March Saturday so memorable. And Bridget, a girl from Winketauk, had gotten permission from her parents to visit Kingsmount for the entire afternoon.

In celebration of the sun, Bridget brought a tennis racket, so we went to the tennis courts. Nets weren't up and patches of ice clung stubbornly along the borders. We rallied back and forth, imagining as much of a net as we needed, she floating lightly in a long beige skirt, not awkward even when missing the ball entirely. I didn't care if we ever hit the ball, just so she'd keep floating that way. And then there I went, chasing an errant ball across a patch of ice, tumbling with awkward embarrassment, tearing both my sweater and my hand and swearing softly through my teeth as I sat up in a puddle. I've never relished an injury so much as that one; it meant we didn't have to play any more.

We picked our way along through wet fields flashing in sun. Down by the brook, not far from where I'd waded out six months before, Bridget let me kiss her. Her face was set with fate-heavy acceptance, not very different from Saul's as he ran along beyond the stream a few minutes later.

We were standing in a little hollow beneath an oak, and he never spotted us. Mud streaked his legs as he drove on, nothing triumphant in the struggle, only a resignation akin to Bridget's. He ran slowly, his strong legs straining, mired even as he ran. Bridget watched him silently, distantly. I kissed her again, pulling her close, wrapping her in my arms. Her breath was warm, and she kissed me too, and when after a long time we drew apart for breath and to share a shy smile, Saul had disappeared.

In the fall the promised magic fulfilled itself. Alumni, students and local fans filled our little stadium for every game. We'd never seen such crowds before, especially for a team that couldn't win. They wanted to win; if there'd been any resentment of Saul the year before, his teammates atoned with new eagerness. Not four or five but a dozen times a game, he'd launch those beautiful, desperate, doomed passes, arching them down field to receivers who dropped them, or turned the wrong way, or slipped tumbling in the mud. But once or twice during a game, a pass clicked for a touchdown, or by sheer force of will he tore himself free and into the clear. The stands were never very noisy; there was little enough reason for noise. Everyone waited almost breathlessly for the brilliant, sparse magic. Saul's friends, fans, teammates, all savored the simple fact, which any fool could see, that not a prayer to heaven or hell would help this team win.

He relished the adoration, dismissed the sympathy. I don't think he ever understood that the adoration grew more intense as the defeats mounted. He didn't blame the team; they were in some way incidental. He accepted it all, receiving the attentions of local girls and other fans, and driving himself because he thought he had to, that victory was what they coveted—when that was really incidental.

By the middle of the season he'd stopped riding into town with me on weekends, so I quit as well; I didn't see much point in going alone. We each had our own room by this time, and I'd run into him. Sometimes we'd talk. I could tell he wasn't sleeping well, and I tried to conjure some of the pressure to share, but that gratified me more than it helped him.

The final game of the season was played at home. Despite a week of heavy frost, the stands were packed as at the other games, and as quiet and expectant. No one really thought we'd win, especially since University School had one of the best teams in our region. But maybe the cold evened things out. Kingsmount played solid football for the first time all year, Saul threw a short pass for a touchdown and the score was tied at halftime.

The excitement ebbed as it grew colder, or seemed to, during the fifteen-minute break. Bridget and I had a heavy blanket over our knees and another wrapped around our shoulders, but her eyes watered with the cold and I could feel her shivering.

University School scored soon after receiving the next kick-off—they ran hard and fast, right at our defense, which couldn't settle itself. Down by a touchdown, Kingsmount—Saul—got the ball back.

On the second play from scrimmage, he dropped back to pass, his wrist by his ear ready to throw, when the receiver slipped and fell. Saul hesitated and they hit him. Two linemen hit him from the back; he never saw them coming. A ragged cheer drifted across from the other side of the field. He was groggy, and he'd hurt his hands. They looked stiff and clumsy, aching with cold. Twice he fumbled the snap from center, and then trotted slowly from the field to let the defense take over.

Our team stopped University School dead, didn't allow them a yard. It was that way for the rest of the game. Kingsmount playing wildly over their heads. The same thing happened on offense. The team blocked and ran, and blocked again. Their desperation gave way to a kind of frenzied joy. They wanted to win the game for Saul—but just as he couldn't win before then without them, they couldn't win now. He didn't fumble again, but neither could he throw. He tried, lifting the ball and shoving it forward into the air where it fluttered and dropped lamely onto the frozen ground. Again and then again he tried, and then he quit trying. He ran with the ball, and handed it to other backs to run. It wasn't enough. Kingsmount lost to a shaken University School by that one touchdown.

I didn't run into him for a week, not until the Headmaster's Formal, because I was busy with a new production. By the time Bridget and I arrived at the dance, he was well on his way with both the punch and his date from the girl's school thirty miles up the road. She was lovely and a little drunk. They were shuffling in place in a dark corner of the dining hall when we discovered them. Touching his arm, I whispered in his ear, "You sure set them up for next year."

The smile he gave me was drunk and vacant. "Don't tell me about next year," he said so loudly that people glanced our way. I smelled whiskey on his breath as he shoved me back a step. I don't know if he did it intentionally, or if he stumbled, or if he was too drunk to realize he'd done it at all. I was angry—I didn't deserve that—and Bridget and I crossed back to the other side of the hall.

The cold snap hadn't eased; actually, it had deepened. I don't know what the temperature was that night. Cold enough. And I don't know if Saul got what he wanted from his date, but they were at the bus on time with all the other girls. Then, loaded with bourbon, he went for a walk across the estate.

I heard him when he woke Frye, our housemaster. We all did. He beat on the door with his elbow and shoulder because he'd been inside long enough—it was after five—for his hands and feet to thaw and ache. I went out to see what was going on. He was crying, almost wailing, and he still wasn't sober.

The housemaster and I went to the hospital with Saul. By the time we got there we had to hold him by the arms because of the pain. Even drunk he was so strong we could hardly hang on, and if I can't translate it, I can hear him wailing. They took most of his fingers and two toes from each foot.

Three days passed before I went back to the hospital. What with his parents and the team, he had people enough around him.

One night I got permission to borrow the keys to the school's red pickup truck. The heater didn't work—as far as I knew, it had never worked—and the damn thing, old as it was, wouldn't do much better than thirty-five.

Only twenty minutes were left of visiting hours when I got there. I'd wanted it that way. His door was on the crack; I didn't knock, I nudged it open and slipped into the room.

One of the local girls who'd met the team bus a year ago was with him.

Saul didn't glance at me—he was sick of visitors. His hands were jammed beneath the blankets, his cheeks and forehead flushed, a film of sweat on his lip. The girl flashed a nervous, grateful smile. I'd set her free. She leaned over the bed and whispered. His eyes leaped my way as she kissed him.

"Teddy, you bastard—why didn't you come before?" he asked after the girl left the room.

"I was here the first night."

"Yeah." He closed his eyes. The sweat shone on his flushed skin. "But you should've come back before."

I stepped close to the bed. I wanted to shake his hand, grip it for support and comfort—as if I'd forgotten what this was all about. I caught myself. I placed my hand awkwardly on his shoulder.

"Hey, Teddy Shannon—know what?" His eyes were closed and he wore a terrible smile. "I'm glad."

I couldn't breathe, every muscle in my chest and throat and thighs was tense, and visiting hours were over, and I didn't understand, and I couldn't say anything, and I wanted to run outside.

"Look what I've done to myself, Teddy." He took a breath, his jaw clenched. "God knows, I'm glad. God *knows* I'm glad."

He didn't open his eyes to look at me until I'd bent down and kissed his forehead because I couldn't kiss his lips. His skin was hot. I tasted its sweat, and when he did look at me the smile was sad if still triumphant, mocking me gently, and grateful too.

In January, Saul reported to school with the rest of us, but I saw little more of him than I had before. The dramatic society owned even more of my time because I'd just been elected president. One thing: those weekend visits of ours to church and synagogue began again with the new year. He came by without warning one Saturday morning and shook me by the shoulder until I was awake.

"Come on—we're gonna be late," he said, and walked out again. The next Sunday he woke me less gently.

Saul spent a lot of time by himself that spring. For long hours he'd hike across the estate or hide with his books in a classroom. He hated to have us see him fumble with the pages.

I wrote to him twice that summer, but I didn't expect an answer. He'd have had to ask someone to write for him. I discovered what he was about only when I returned for our last year at Kingsmount, and learned he'd been there for two weeks. I damned him, but not to his face.

Over the summer, he'd taught himself to punt at the same time he was learning to run again. We saw him rock his body and burst into the football as he warmed up before the first game. An hour early the stands were filling—word had passed. They'd come to see if there'd be any magic left. Twice in the first half he trotted onto the field to kick the ball away, and he still carried himself with the same confidence. Or better. It wasn't confidence so much as an intent willingness to grapple with what was to come.

Twice he rocked into the ball with a soft, studied fierceness, and it arched soaring over the heads of receivers downfield. In the silence we heard slap as he met leather, and then, twice, came a long slow swell of cheering they couldn't give him a year before. But there was something wrong with all of it. He doesn't owe them this, I thought. It was lovely and it was terrible all at once. And I wished he'd fail. I wanted this to end now before it became unbearable, whether for Saul or for me didn't matter. The cheering hung in the air, richer the second time than the first.

He didn't have to kick again until the fourth quarter. He ran onto the field, and some of the fans were cheering already, no longer hushed and anticipating magic, but demanding it.

It wasn't Saul's fault. The ball came high, over his head, and he leapt for it. He and the ball hung in counterpoise, battling each other.

The football glanced off his hands. He stumbled when he landed and spun round to pick it up, ready to kick or run, but it was too late. The defense broke past the line and dropped him. It took two of them to do it. He ran off the field, his head up as he came back to the bench. They all stood and cheered, his teammates too, and that was the first time I cried. I'd wanted him to fail, he had, they were yelling, I was angry, I cried.

After the games he turned in his equipment. He spoke to the coach quietly, in private, and came back up the dorm to read on in Virgil. A kid in high school, and he was reading Virgil.

He told me about it, hinting and bobbing indirectly the next morning because it was the week for church. We didn't have much chance to talk then, and I didn't know what to ask or say.

This year, he wouldn't let us skip our weekend trips to town, especially on Saturdays. In our weekends together he hadn't tried to teach me—nothing more than a few words of Hebrew. By then, I didn't feel so out of place in the synagogue, but there was more to it that autumn. Every few minutes he'd glance up from the prayerbook I held for both of us, and he would become angry if my attention had strayed Penitent, I'd do my best. He wanted me to understand, to belong. I didn't mind. It was enough that he wanted so much to share this, and with me.

During the fall, he was cool and calm and friendly to everyone. And sometimes he'd glance up at me out of that prayerbook and not be angry, but scared—almost shivering with it. He'd already got beyond feeling sorry for himself, but I think he was afraid of wanting something very much again, as much as he'd wanted to play football. We're different. I envy him, always have. I've never wanted anything that much.

The Headmaster's Formal was two weeks later than the year before. I'd been seeing Bridget for nearly two years and still had to take her home by midnight. We were so intent on making the most of dinner in town and three hours of dancing at school, it didn't occur to me that I hadn't seen Saul until he knocked at my door a little after one.

Instead of a tux, he was wearing a baggy green sweater his sister had knit while he was in the hospital. "Let's get out of here, Teddy," he said with a grin.

I didn't have to be persuaded. I tore off my rented dinner jacket, pulled on a heavy sweater and grabbed the keys to the red pickup truck. That damn truck. It took us twenty minutes to get it started in the cold, worrying every minute about being caught, but we got away free and clear. A bearing was loose in the drive shaft, and at thirty-five the whole thing began to shake like the apocalypse.

"I promised myself something like this—should've done it before," he said.

I shot him a surprised glance. "You know I'd do this anytime you want."

He nodded, and I could see a smile in the darkness. "Can't let you do too much for me, Shannon," he replied.

"Shit," I said.

At the all-night store, the big question was whether to buy a bottle of good muscatel or two cheaper bottles. We took two, and a loaf of bread to soak it up. With nowhere else to go, we rattled our way back to a country road near Kingsmount. We figured the wine and our own breath would keep us warm.

Since I had to open the bottles, Saul tore the bread. He presented me with a piece while I handed him the bottle. He sniffed it, took a short swallow. Our breath frosted in the stillness. We didn't talk much.

Before our muscatel—so sweet we screwed up our eyes and winced with each swallow—had much chance to get me drunk, it put me to sleep. I was so groggy by the time both bottles were empty, he had to drag me to the other side of the cab, crawl across and drive us out. And when the pickup was back in the garage he half-dragged, half-carried me up to the dorm.

My window wasn't locked, and I was able to grab onto it and pull as he pushed me through. We didn't switch on the light, though no one was up to catch us at that hour. Once I was on the bed he drew up a blanket to cover me.

"Get some sleep, Sport," he whispered.

"We finish the wine?" I asked.

I woke up Saturday morning at a little past six, groggy, mouth dry, tongue swollen. For a while I lay on my back, and when I finally rolled out of bed to get some water I spotted Saul's old velvet case with his prayer shawl on my desk. I got the water and came back. I didn't think much about it at first, but as I tried to fall asleep again it nagged. We weren't due at the synagogue for hours. Why would he bring the shawl and leave it with me?

Ten minutes later, I stumbled out of bed again—still wearing the crumpled dress shirt and trousers—and hurried off down the hall to his room. The door was open, but he wasn't there and he wasn't in the shower. Dopey from the night before and confused, I was suddenly worried too. I checked the dining hall; its doors were locked. Back in my room, I picked up the velvet case and stared at it hard, as if that would clear my head. I guess Saul had emptied my pockets before I got on the bed, because my wallet and change and room keys were also on the desk. But not the keys to the pickup.

I pulled on a sweater and ran. A half-inch of snow had fallen since I'd gone to bed, and it was still snowing.

The truck coughed and sputtered, backing unwillingly out of the garage. I rushed up, breathless, and wrenched open the door. Saul switched off the engine and stared at me, angry but not surprised. A full duffle bag sat next to him.

"Where are you going?" I shouted, panting.

He shook his head, saying nothing. He climbed down out the truck and faced me.

"Where you going?" I said again, and pointed to the duffle.

"Gotta go," he answered with a shrug. Angry, his eyes challenging, he stared at me.

"With my keys to the truck?"

"That's right," he said.

I stepped forward and thrust my hand into the cab for the keys. Saul knocked my arm aside. And I hit him, quick and sharp, swinging around with my other hand, catching him on the side of his head. Before I could pull away he swiped with the back of his hand, knocking me back and down in the snow. I came at him again, I swung, he blocked it with his arm and caught me with a blow to the chest. I sank into the snow again, gasping.

Saul hesitated, watching me until he was satisfied. Then he climbed up into the truck.

"Stop," I called in a whisper. He shook his head. The red pickup snorted, nearly stalled, but never quite died as he drove away.

They found it the next day at the train station in town, a couple of hours after I'd told Frye he was gone. Three days later, he called his parents from Boston and they let us know.

He went to Boston—my town—but it was a different town for him. Two years later, I spotted him on the street. By the time I was off the streetcar he'd disappeared. He had got himself into college, after waiting and working for a year, without having graduated from Kingsmount. I guess his Latin was that good.

I kept the velvet case he'd left in my room. During that spring at Kingsmount I even carried it to the synagogue in Winketauk once or twice, though I never wore the prayer shawl. I knew that some time or other, when the time was right, he'd come for it.

Recollections

As his car wound up and over a small rise, Philip Wyatt caught a first glimpse of Dartmoor swelling above the quilt of Devonshire farms. His throat tightened with a brief flush of the exhilaration he'd been banking on. But there was also something disorienting in this raw glint of wilderness. He'd expected to find the moor familiar as an old friend, changed perhaps around the edges but the same in all essentials. Yet already the hills surging before him seemed too sharp and severe, unchanged, unrecognizable. Squinting against the afternoon glare, he wondered whether Miriam Prothro and her mother Helen, the old friends he hoped to find in Exeter, would seem so strange.

The road dipped beside a stream. Around a bend to the left he rediscovered a lane, little more than a path really, that wound its way from the heavy vegetation along the river up to the orangish heath and patches of grey stone high on the moor's scalp. But if Philip was pleased with himself (better than twenty years and to find the path at first try!), still, with nearly every glance he felt this lingering disorientation, a whiff almost of vertigo, as if what he remembered so vividly refused to accommodate the actual landscape about him.

The small car he'd rented at Heathrow bucked against the slope. Each jolt rattled him against a physical immanence of stone and moss and bramble that he'd described, and in describing transformed, in some dozen of his stories for American magazines over the years. He'd been faithful to memories of two and a half years here in the English west country, as faithful as the demands of a story allowed. But he now began to realize that the cumulative effect of all the small compromises and shadings he'd made in those tales was that his memories had come to inhabit quite a different place from the moor surrounding him at this moment.

By the time he reached a rolling plateau the climb had left him breathless. He pulled off onto a natural shoulder at the edge of a great stone outcrop and stepped out of the car. A sharp wind ripped across the exposed highland. Chilled in an instant, he fumbled at his jacket zipper, peevish with his own frailty.

Only an occasional scene had actually been set on the moor, of course. But this wilderness hovered always in the background of the broader precincts of Devon and Cornwall where he'd set other stories from exile. For twenty years he'd managed to rekindle his memories so that some trace survived the translation into language, like the flinty grit that passed for soil here under a thin rind of moss. (But not for months, not about the moor, not about anything.) And now he'd run himself smack against a more immediate truth: the grain of the rock, the spine of the gorse, the honing wind. They existed with a density that defied both his memory and his description. Rarely had he been forced to confront just how far language had failed him, how a ragged horizon and an acrid scent in the breeze could mock his profession.

He walked around the car. The high sky, an immense sky, was pale, greyer than blue. A marrow-numbing chill had him shivering already, fingers numb in his pockets. He thought again of Miriam, of how he'd brought her here the first time—a bus to the village along the river and a hike up to this same rocky *tor* where they perched with cheese and bread. She was wearing a fisherman's smock. Faded blue, almost periwinkle. Philip closed his eyes for an instant—he could taste that blue. This was the kind of memory, jagged, fresh, unsummoned, that had been sweeping over him since he'd begun to recover from his illness. The powerful desire he'd conceived (while still plugged in and dripped into in a hospital bed) to revisit the English west country had culled a curiosity, a desire to see Miriam again too. And the imminent possibility suddenly frightened him.

The town was more faithful to his memories, even though superficial change was visible everywhere. New franchise shops—boutiques they were now—had replaced old ones, probably into the fifth or sixth generation. Along the High Street off-track betting parlors snuggled comfortably. Bright lights, video screens, plastic parquet: the general shabbiness had struck root in the town's shabby resurrection after the war.

A few things, however, he'd counted on to survive. And yes, there, ahead in the dusk he made out the hanging sign with the leaping white hart. The inn was one of a scattered handful of buildings that had survived the German bombing. Its most ancient rooms formed a misshapen warren, dark and snug, while the main trunk had grown by incremental branches and twists, like one of the stubborn oaks along the margins of town. As a young man Philip could afford only the odd pint of beer here. But on this visit he intended to take a room and walk the town properly as part of his convalescence.

One of the better rooms was indeed available, a uniformed steward informed him. Would Mr. Wyatt be caring for dinner as well? The question smote Philip with weariness, as if the exhaustion of the long journey had been trailing behind and only caught him at this instant. His knees softened. He leaned with one hand on the back of a chair, afraid that tears might come and shame him (as they had five weeks ago when he was delivered home and couldn't manage the porch steps by himself). *Christ*, he hated this, the helplessness, the childishness of it. No, many thanks, no dinner. He allowed the steward to take his bag and lead him to the room. Soon he lay in bed and waited for sleep.

✳

Small surprise that October should fling sheets of rain against his window in the early morning. Still groggy and not terribly dismayed by the weather, Philip took two cups of coffee downstairs, skimming a different newspaper with each. And, small surprise, by the time he finished his breakfast the clouds had scudded clear.

Late in the morning he crossed the street and followed an ancient walled lane between modern shops. It narrowed, twisted, and opened abruptly onto the cathedral close. The church sprawled heavy, grey, inert, a handsome fossil, its two squat towers foreshortened tusks. Deferring respects until later, Philip took the short cut across the close.

On the other side of town he headed up the long hill that rose from the river. On its slope perched the redbrick university, bordered on the east by houses also red brick, the grass in their gardens trimmed close as billiard cloth. But it was the smell he'd been smelling all morning, a telltale whiff of tar from the road and smoke from a coal fire—now, standing on a street corner, he was suddenly aware of it—that made this place and his own presence real, an aroma fainter than he remembered even though until this moment he'd never recalled it. For an instant he was all of twenty-three again, lonely and enchanted by this country that was half fairytale, half grubbily reeling from a war decades past.

As he halted on that busy corner, a lorry lumbering in the wrong-right lane swiped him with its roar. And the trailing plume of diesel exhaust swept away the sensation of youth too quickly, between breaths—but already he'd been carried across a threshold that had balked him since Heathrow. No more doubts about where he was; nothing here of any consequence had changed. *He* had changed. A stitch in his side warned him to slow his pace.

By habit as much as plan, he turned away from the university gates and into a certain street. Several blocks up and off to one side lay a quiet cul-de-sac, and yes, as he strolled by and halted he could make out a certain cottage tucked behind a row of lilac bushes. Presenting as tidy a face as ever, its brick was painted white. A bay window reflected the low autumn sun.

His breathing quickened. His blood beat in his throat and temples. He snorted sarcastically at this body of his, behaving like an adolescent or a very old man indeed. Since his illness he'd grown more alert to it as something mechanical, unpredictable, an object over which he had limited control at best. He hesitated another moment, then opened the gate and rapped at the door.

After a few seconds it swung open and facing him, inquisitive then delighted, were the grey-green eyes and high brow of a woman he surely knew. A sharp whip of joy—and disbelief—snapped through his limbs. How was it possible that Helen Prothro hadn't aged twenty months in twenty years? She might have welcomed him for tea the day before.

For her part, hesitation lasted only an instant. "Philip!" she cried. But as her eyes flickered over his face, he saw her surprise at his hollow cheeks, his darkened eyes, his thin grey hair. In that instant she was smiling the same smile as other friends and family in recent weeks who hadn't been prepared.

Yet as she reached for his hand something in her eyes gave the secret away. Comprehension arrived with a fresh dizzying wave of disorientation. *Miriam*, not Helen. He grinned stupidly. But Miriam was suddenly her mother's age (the age he'd known Helen Prothro) and she was his age too. Her brown hair was streaked with grey and drawn back in a ponytail. His brain stiffly sorted the paradoxes even as she hugged him. He was ashamed of his own confusion and hoped she hadn't guessed.

"You got my card?" he murmured. "This all, this trip—it came together at the last minute. I just took the chance you or your mother would be here. Last I heard, you were on your way again from Australia. Or was it Japan?"

She nodded and tugged at his hand. "It only came in yesterday's post—I've been breathless ever since."

He held fast for a moment, feeling lame and embarrassed. "Is your mother home too?"

"She died two years ago," Miriam said. "That's why I came back, to see after her things. I haven't managed to get away again, at least not yet."

Philip glanced past her shoulder into the house. Not that he doubted, not that he didn't believe her. But he was keeping the fact of death and the treacherous gulf of sadness safely at bay. Far away, distant, distant, he tucked the notion that Helen Prothro was dead. He nodded. "I'm sorry—I should've found out, should've known."

"How could you? It's my fault for not letting you know." She tugged again at his arm. "Come in—I've just put coffee on."

He followed her like a naughty child led by the hand.

Whatever the faithfulness of its appearance outside, the cottage's interior had been dramatically altered. Familiar objects—a reading chair, the sideboard—were rearranged or reupholstered, scattered among new pieces, many from the east. By the fireplace a black marble Krishna balanced on one foot. Shadow puppets danced along a wall.

While Miriam poured the coffee, he settled onto an ottoman tucked into the bay window. "I'm sorry I didn't get in touch to warn you sooner. A whim carried me away—like the old me, isn't it?—and everything's been a rush and a jumble since. I don't know why I even expected to find you here."

"I should have written when Mother died, but it had been so long. I wasn't sure I had a recent address."

"You're not one to talk," he said, stirring his coffee and smiling. "I don't remember you keeping me up to date on your wanderings across the globe."

"I kept meaning to, Philip—as soon as something seemed more settled, more permanent. But there was Sydney and then Tokyo, and meanwhile we'd fallen rather out of touch. Didn't I let you know about the new investment research I was doing in Tokyo?"

He was nodding as she explained—yes, he now remembered, there'd been a Christmas card or two both ways, others returned for incorrect address. But he was also watching her, noticing how she'd come to resemble her mother in the jerky flutters of a hand, in her grey-green eyes. The first time she'd brought him home for tea he'd had to confront that look of hers—theirs—a knowing, wry little smile that poked through the writerly persona he was attempting to fashion for himself.

Miriam he'd met at the university pub where they both worked in the evenings, he to support his morning hours writing in the library (with American bravado he'd snagged a carrel by the windows though he had no official connection to the university), she more for the principle of the work than for extra money while a student. On his way back to his bedsit in the afternoon, Philip took to strolling past Mrs. Prothro's. After that first visit as Miriam's guest, however, it was never a matter of easy tea and cakes. Helen Prothro would put him right to work peeling apples or weeding her garden. Always there was a project, some goal she'd set for herself (and caught him up in too). Reward was hot cider and cinnamon. And over the mug he'd tell them stories, stories he'd heard or read about, stories he made up, improbable, impossible, wild stories. They *laughed.*

Miriam was sitting across from him in a big chintz chair, and she poured more coffee from a stainless-steel thermos. She seemed very thin in her denim skirt and loose blouse, too thin. Her longish fingers looked as though they worried each other.

He ate a biscuit and then another. He was enjoying simply looking at her. Her smile flickered again and then tightened. "You've been ill," she said.

He shrugged, glanced away and back. "Yeah—that all happened pretty quickly too. The doctors went ga-ga over an exotic tumor my body worked up. They *adore* my pancreas." He smiled wryly. "They're miffed with me now for going into remission."

She nodded but didn't press him for more. Not for the first time he wished she weren't so reticent, so mindful of not prying, so damn English. He wanted to tell her more, the whole story, the fears and wretchedness even in victory, wanted her to press him. But after ten minutes—after much less time than that—they'd already adjusted to sitting here together, yin-and-yang of an old fit, frustrations and all.

"In some ways, Philip," Mrs. Prothro had declared one day when Miriam wasn't home, "you are a very stupid boy." She'd just pinned the corner of a damp pillowcase to the line. He was squatting ten feet away planting bulbs. Startled, he swiveled on a heel to glance up at her.

"Why do you suppose my daughter happens by the student lounge just when you're having your sandwich? Everyday no less."

"On purpose?" That it never occurred to him embarrassed him. He rallied. "Of *course* she comes by then—that's the place to catch me. It's not like we have time to talk while we're washing glasses in the pub."

"Oh, well yes, you're *friends*—which isn't what I'm talking about at all."

He rose and scraped the dirt from his fingers. Annoyed, baffled, he stared at her. Given her usual delicacy about such things, she'd astonished him. "What are you talking about?" he snapped. "What else can you expect? Wait a second. Am I forgetting something or didn't you throw an engagement party last spring? *I* wasn't invited. What, was your idea that I'd show up on a white horse like Ivanhoe, spoil the party, sweep her away? You've got to be kidding."

Helen Prothro sighed, conceding his point. "I don't know why Miriam has handled her engagement so poorly. She and Ian began seeing each other long before you arrived, of course. And when he went up to Oxford an engagement seemed, well, inevitable. Everyone, their friends, expected it. I don't think she's ever really wanted to marry Ian. But she knew I was skeptical. And she is stubborn—that was reason enough for her to carry through with that silly party. Ian's quite a little swine as a matter of fact."

"Can you manage a walk?" asked Miriam, startling him.

He couldn't tell whether she'd noticed how he'd drifted away. "Just what I need," he said, rousing himself and tugging his jacket back on while she fetched a scarf and one of her mother's old-fashioned wool capes.

The afternoon had turned cold and blustery. Miriam set off quickly and led the way out to the main road. Rather than crossing over to the university grounds, she turned up the hill. With most traffic swinging in at the main gate, the road narrowed sharply.

Philip was already puffing. He caught at her cape. "Can we take it a little easier?" he called, winded.

She halted as if scalded. "Good lord—what am I thinking? Seeing you has me swimming a bit." She hooked her arm through his for a gentler stroll.

"I've read some of your stories, you know," she said loudly against the wind.

"How'd you manage that?" His own alarm surprised him. And then he remembered. "Oh, you mean the ones I sent you early on."

"No—well those too, naturally. No, I mean some of your later stories. Do you remember Judith? Or Harrie? They both moved to the States while I was away. One or the other sends back a story when she happens across it. Judith has sent several—she sees them all the time. But the point is, they're wonderful. You're a wonderful writer, Philip. I've wanted to tell you that for a long time—you used to want it so and work so hard."

She glanced slyly at him as they slowly climbed the hill. "Do you know, when I'm reading them I sometimes feel I'm a detective, or that I'm in on a secret. They're not always *true* are they?—the ones you set over here. You really do change an awful lot."

"That's why it's called fiction," he snapped more brusquely than he'd intended. "I've never pretended to be a historian." This conversation he'd had before, and always resented it. For years his father had held his mining of family chronicles against him. Though then the crime was that he hadn't changed enough, that the world would be privy to dark secrets or, at the very least, that some defamed cousin might recognize herself in the pages of a magazine.

She was shaking her head. "I'll be thinking *I know these people—I know this story.* There's such excitement in that. And then they'll do something wrong. Not wrong for the story. Not that at all. Just different from the way it happened. But I guess that's why you're such a successful writer."

He bridled at the compliment. Best intentions or not, she was chafing a sore point raw. "Hey, look," he said, "the story dictates any changes—I don't set out to do it. Besides, it's a long time since I wrote anything you could recognize. Anything." He left it at that.

As they rounded a slow bend the crest of the hill drew close. Beyond and below, the country opened before them, one hill disappearing gently into the folds of another. A herd of dairy cattle perched high across the way.

A sharp gust of wind released a hard and driving shower. They ducked for cover into a stand of oaks. The trees clustered close enough to provide some shelter, though most of their leaves had already fallen. It seemed the most natural thing in the world for Philip to put his arm around her from behind and draw her close. She didn't resist, exactly. It was more that she acquiesced, allowed him to.

The rain in her hair and on the wool cape conjured a potent scent. Tucking his head closer to her ear he breathed again, igniting fresh memories and longings that had to do with her, principally her, but with other women he'd loved as well. He wanted to stand like this for hours—he also wanted to rush her away to the inn and spend the evening in a long, gentle, furious bout of lovemaking. He felt excited simply for feeling up to it.

She didn't move, not to burrow closer, not to squirm free. Those damn cows on the far ridge distracted her. She might almost have forgotten him. Slighted, he drew his head back.

And that little distance, inches, allowed him to see. The tilt of her head or the arch of her back against him—something—gave it away. How wrong he'd been. Far from ignoring him, Miriam was upset and struggling not to give way. Finding him on the doorstep, the flood of memories, some combination, had all but swept her away. He was touched. He was pleased.

In another moment she slipped from his arm and tied the scarf more securely on her head. "Looks as though the worst's blown past. Why don't we go a little farther—or must you get back?" She said this back over her shoulder, yet the glimpse of her eyes made his heart sink, his presumption collapse. Though she tried to disguise it, the fierceness he spied was anything but a weepy joy: she was furious with him.

He touched her arm. "What's the matter, Urchin?"

She winced. "I never did like that name, if you must know. Urchins may be Disney characters for you, but we don't think of them as all that cute. At my age it's ridiculous."

He was shadowboxing an adversary that was quick, elusive, nowhere to be seen. "Okay. Got it. So at least tell me what you haven't forgiven."

She shrugged.

"Something new or old? Christ, Miriam, you visited me twice in the States without any problem."

Her eyes snapped to his. "That was different, wasn't it? It wasn't here again. You were married the first time. I had a chap in tow, the second. My mother wasn't dead."

The catalogue chilled him.

She grabbed his hand and tugged him along onto the road once more. "You were such a bastard, you might as well know. I'd forgotten. I loved you and you were a bastard there at the end, and then you wrote a story about it that got it all wrong."

Philip let her lead him along for several paces. Those years suddenly seemed ancient history. *You are a stupid boy*, Helen Prothro had declared.

"Who knows—maybe you've written about it more than once," Miriam was saying as they marched along the wet road. "But what galled me about the version I saw wasn't the little superficial changes. You know, the names and place and background—all that. But you made it the girl's fault. You made the sour ending *my* fault."

"I don't remember a story like that," he said.

"You have her manipulate the poor boy into finally confessing he loves her, only so she can whip up some jealousy from her fiancé. That's the essence of it."

Her cheeks were flushed from the wind. Pink cheeks, greying hair, an angry mouth. Suddenly this was someone he didn't know at all, had never known: neither the mother nor the girl he'd once thought he loved, but a strange creature, as frightening as those stone outcrops on the moor. He felt a powerful urge simply to turn away and hurry back to town alone.

"If you like, I'll tell you the truth about what happened," she was saying. "You spoiled a good friendship, that's what you did. You knew I was engaged to Ian, and all of a sudden you start cooing at me and touching me, there at the end, when you only had a few weeks left, when you knew you were going home."

"But you didn't love that jerk—that never had a chance."

She wheeled on him. "What right did you have to think that, or to act on it, if you were planning to rush away free?"

Off she strode again, he tagging after. "I remember a night in the pub." Her tone shifted abruptly, a meld of accusation and wistfulness. "After closing, when George and Winnie were out front checking the till. I was scrubbing glasses in the back room and you'd just fetched in a new cartload. Do you remember? You ploshed a handful of mugs into the water and touched my arm and you kissed me. The first time in all that time. My hands were soapy and you had soap and water all over your shirt when Winnie came in. Did *she* give us a look."

His fists were driven deep into his pockets, shoulders hunched more sharply than the wind demanded. Philip nodded and smiled. He hoped it didn't look as stiff as it felt. It wasn't that he didn't remember. It was just that he didn't believe it happened quite that way. Wasn't the scene one he'd all but invented for some story or other? Maybe she'd seen it there. How much of this was history, how much fiction?

"Here, we've come far enough," she announced abruptly. "I don't want to wear you out." Without waiting for a reply, she turned off the road towards a cattle gate. "This gives us a nice shortcut home." She ushered him through before her and onto a common path that cut an angle back to town.

Closing the gate, she took up the thread once more, an invisible spirit behind him speaking into the wind. "That was lovely, the night in the bar. If only you'd flown back to America right then. But I remember the last night too, which turned out pretty badly, you leaving for good in the morning. And then you wrote a story about it, and that was even worse.

"Did you have any idea how long I spent cooking your farewell dinner? The night before and all day it was. Half-a-dozen friends coming to the house, and Mother wouldn't lift a finger to help—she insisted on being a guest too. We had such a lovely dinner."

"*That* I remember," he said triumphantly. "Roast beef and carrots. An incredible pudding. Meant the world to me. You were terrific."

"It was late when everyone left. Mother had already kissed you goodbye and gone to bed. We stayed up, you and I, and we talked. And then I gave you a lift back to your bedsit. The seven-thirty train to catch and you weren't even packed yet. And we're sitting in the car outside and you kiss me again. But you're not saying anything. What do you want? I said. You know, you said. All right, I said. That's not good enough, you said. I *want* to, I said."

She halted abruptly in the lee of a hedge. She'd plucked a bit of vine and was tearing at it with her fingers.

Stop, he wanted to say. For a single instant her voice had conjured a girl's face reaching up to him, vivid, already darkening, gone beyond retrieval. *Don't do this—I remember*, he wanted to say. *I loved you then.*

"So up we went to your flat. Middle of May and it was still freezing up there. You were out of your clothes in no time and tugging at mine, dragging me under the pile of covers. Hurry, hurry—you were in such a rush." She stopped for a moment, tossed the green scrap away, glanced at the small slate-grey clouds against a darkening sky. Twilight was advancing rapidly. "You didn't take any time at all. Not any. I didn't feel bad about it then, because I wanted you too. But maybe I did believe that all you wanted, really, was to have done it at last, a memory or souvenir to take away with you. Something to store for a rainy day."

"I was a boy," he said lamely. "I didn't know what the hell I was doing when it came to sex."

The lane wasn't wide enough along here for the two of them to walk comfortably abreast. Silence followed him as he set off again. But he knew she was close on his heels. That urge to rush away from her swelled once more. His teeth ached with it. And he was angry too, disenchanted and angry, indulging a good, free, hot indignation that she should spring this on him after so long, as though it could matter anymore.

Yet the wicked slant she cast on the tale, the way she'd shaped her own memories—he knew that wasn't what so vexed him (though saddened him, yes). He could take exception to this or that, certainly to her ultimate verdict, but such was the nature of the game, as he well knew. Whatever quibbles he might have, whatever distortions her history might be guilty of, the scene she painted was vivid. Her words carried the undeniable resonance of a storyteller's truth. He saluted it silently.

His own version was different of course. Imminent departure had lent an urgency, a sharpness to the taste of her dinner and the awkward eagerness of limbs in his bed. Yearning, fresh love, closure all were sealed magically into a single evening. For years he'd drawn liberally on the memory—the trace of salt on her skin, the incandescent surprise of her nipple rising to him, the sadness of dawn—transmuting the memory's truth, its energy, into the lifeblood of new tales.

Breathing heavily again, a stitch in his side, he slowed his pace. His shirt clung to him under the jacket. Miriam had fallen a few yards behind, apparently content not to catch up. His initial comforting resentment at her accusations had slowly dampened, the urge to flee grown slack, abandoning him on a wet path in deepening shadows, chilled and lonely and older than he'd been.

Inadvertently, Miriam had brought him to see the steep price he'd paid, not for any particular sin twenty years past, but for having drawn *too* liberally on those potent memories. He'd been so cavalier—worrying them, tearing at them, twisting, honing them. Somewhere along the way he'd forfeited the quick of that evening she described. What had actually happened and what he'd invented later for the sake of a good story were jumbled beyond repair. He could only piece together broken shards as if he'd stumbled on a heap in someone else's album.

Her car. His bedsit. Had she really said that? Had he been so thoughtless? The images and sensations, the shadows of love, lay far away, someone else's story, muted by years, mediated by fictions, recollected but not recoverable.

A fresh wave of disgust surged and fell back, tearing anchors loose and leaving him adrift. Inertia alone carried him forward along the narrow trail. He had no idea what he was heading towards. No words, no shape, no story. Far from restoring him, this journey was only confirming his fears of barrenness and disconnection. He couldn't even summon rage anymore, a raised fist at his own impotence.

And yet—and yet—he didn't sink to the earth and howl. How ludicrous that would be. His eyes were dry. No tears to seal his humiliation. Scoured and raw, he kept his slow but steady pace along the path. He actually began to feel rather light, a skiff cut loose perhaps, *released*, bow coming around to the swell. Momentum carried him forward, and that was something.

They walked on steadily, one before the other.

As dusk gathered they arrived once more at the fringes of the town. The path emerged between a small market and a wine shop onto a paved road. They were almost home now.

"This way," said Miriam as she stepped to his side. He was glad to have her steer his elbow again.

Despite the occasional car and the cries of invisible children, silence enveloped the two of them. What surprised Philip was the very ease of that silence as they strolled side by side along the pavement. They might have been old conspirators.

An unknown kitchen bragged a rich curry into the air and Philip's stomach growled. He felt ravenous in a way he hadn't for months. The stitch in his side had eased a bit, and he wasn't so terribly exhausted by the trek after all.

Not dismissing the truths he'd encountered on the path, he nevertheless set them aside for the moment. Angst seemed less pressing just now than where they might find an early dinner. Indian would be the thing.

He slapped at his side pocket, at his breast. No pad—he'd lost the habit or it had abandoned him. But there'd be time, if he chose, to scribble some notes, if he chose, before bed.

The Lakeshore Limited

"If only the girl weren't such a fool," Rachel said. A mild flurry swept wearily about them on the platform as passengers boarded the train and porters, a few, struggled half-heartedly with luggage.

Simon nodded and helped her up before him into the coach. He nodded because their granddaughter Mickie was indeed rather a fool, and he was glad that he could agree with his wife at least on this. He wasn't so sure, however, that their worries and this trip and the argument they'd each been bracing for were all simply a result of Mickie's foolishness.

Ever since she was small, Mickie'd had a way of staring at her grandfather Simon with wide-eyed and delighted wonder, equally for bristles he'd missed on his jaw and for his awkward smiles and hugs. Not so long ago, on other visits to Chicago, he'd taken her out along the shore where she insisted on pushing her own stroller. They never made much progress, but that hardly mattered. When little boys came up, she ran back to Simon's pant leg, a devilish grin on her face as she sucked a finger and said not a word to him or to the puzzled or teasing or enchanted boys.

In Chicago what chance has she? he wondered. *If she doesn't marry this one, she'll marry that one—there are too many of them.*

Booking a compartment on the Lakeshore Limited gave Simon and Rachel a chance to drive into town from Jersey for a little shopping and supper before arriving at Grand Central. Ten-thirty at night was certainly a late hour to leave, but at such an hour the station was easy to navigate, and they would be in Chicago well before sundown on Friday. Simon had long ago explained to everyone that Rachel refused to fly if it weren't necessary. He didn't say—he didn't have to—that he himself enjoyed the trains more than most anything since the Dodgers abandoned him and Koufax pitched for them somewhere else.

The pullman seemed very cramped. Their bags sat blocking the door until Simon shoved one before him and into a closet and heaved two others onto a seat. He helped Rachel off with her coat, hung it in the closet, and settled by the window, waiting, while she unpacked her own set of fresh linen. Then he opened the bed so that she could strip and remake it.

Except for the rustling of the bed-clothes it was all very quiet. The late flurry in the station had spent itself, and there was little to see beyond their own reflections in the glass. An occasional porter, his trolley stacked with luggage or newspapers, glided past on the platform.

If Simon didn't actually watch her, focusing beyond even her image in the window, he anticipated Rachel's quick economy. She had never been a pretty woman, not while he'd known her. She was small and fit and a little bit hard. And she'd let her hair go grey, cutting it short and spare.

Once the sheet corners were tugged tight and the blanket secure, Rachel perched across from him, drawing his clasped hands into her own. A little surprised that she'd come to him like this rather than unpack for the night, he smiled a weak smile. The train hadn't moved, and the platform was deserted.

"She's our granddaughter," he said after a few moments.

Rachel was the one who nodded this time.

"Yes?" he said with a shrug. "And she has your name."

She waved the point aside impatiently. "What does that matter, when we call her Mickie? It's such bad taste anyway, Simon—her mother could at least wait until I'm dead to use my name again."

Perhaps because the night was growing late and he was tired, Simon answered sharply. "Why don't you blame your son? It was his idea, of course."

Startled at the angry note in his own voice, he straightened his back but didn't pull his hands free. He glanced warily at his wife. She didn't say anything; her jaw stiffened, but she didn't look at him. For the moment she let it pass.

The train groaned, bucking once backwards, then forwards, drawing slowly through the station and into the night. Rachel was jostled back against her seat and their hands parted. They didn't speak, Simon and Rachel, as they wound clear of the city. A tight whine rose from the tracks as the cars switched and wove, slowing, nearly stopping, heaving forward again. They stared out through the window and waited to breathe and talk with the free and monotonous rhythms of the country.

Once, Simon remembered, he and Mickie had wandered up from the lake into one of the older neighborhoods in Chicago. On a side street he'd discovered a greek market where they sliced her a sliver from a great cake of halvah. The little girl jammed half the crumbly candy into her mouth on the spot, sneaking the rest into the pocket of her smock for safe-keeping while her grandfather wasn't looking. How her mother had laughed when she discovered it! But her father, Eric, Rachel's boy, (not his own, not his own!)—Eric had scolded one or the other of them for the mess; it might as well have been them both.

Manhattan was one long harshly lighted tunnel from which the train slipped all at once into the cool and open darkness beyond the river. Simon switched off the overhead bulb. A reading lamp by the bed cast light enough. While he was up, Rachel fumbled in the closet with another of their bags. She settled by the window again with a flask and two paper cups, and steadying herself cautiously on the edge of the seat, she poured thimbles of brandy. They saluted each other, touching their cups together with a mock solemnity, smiling. Simon saw his wife's smile waver, simply hesitant perhaps or a little bit frightened.

※

Everyone heads the other way, not from Lausanne to Zurich as he does, but as far from this border as possible, as if they all doubt that the boundary of mountains won't crumble away and leave them naked. His compartment is empty, the whole train seems empty, the few other passengers and guards quick and quiet, even stealthy. Perhaps the night makes it seem that way; it is late now and cold. The heat in the coach is crippled, and he huddles deeper into his overcoat. The rocking and shooting of the tracks make the night's silence urgent, a weight that presses on his chest and throat.

As the chill deepens, Simon's initial eagerness at slipping away from Lausanne cloys in his throat—with guilt at having waited so long, with guilt at escaping from his friends when he's sworn not to. Munich is far away yet, and he doesn't want to think about it. But the first border is not so far, and it scares him.

Eyes shut, his head rests back against the seat. From time to time he shivers, but it's not so much the cold. *What else is there for me to do?* he wonders. His eyes are shut tight, feeling hot and dry. *You've chosen already, finally, you'll have to go now*, he answers himself into the jarring silence of the tracks.

Zurich is dark too when they arrive, a different sort of darkness pocked with streetlamps and windows and headlights. Its station is quiet at this hour, yet restless with a late night impotence. The train for Munich will not leave until dawn, and Simon finds a bench in the waiting room where he can doze sitting upright. On one side a young boy in a sailor suit lies stretched out, while on the other half of the bench a salesman sprawls, stinking of sweat and beer, his head resting on a worn and impatiently yellow valise. The waiting room is warm and crowded with the smell of many people asleep.

Before dawn a rough grey burr of light washes through the station. Simon is awake. He's already scorched his tongue on a cup of tea and discovered that his train is running late. *Stop making so much of it, fool,* he thinks, still hungry and not a little grateful that there's time yet. Rubbing a hand across his jaw and shifting on the bench so that his stiff new shirt won't cling, he longs for a hot bath and a chance to shave.

Two sleepy guards shuffle into the waiting room. Clutching his one bag on his knee, Simon doesn't move, not even as they call out his name the first time. But the short Swiss with the mustache and baton barks it out again, annoyed, and Simon rises abruptly, as if he's only just heard, and makes his way through the crowd towards the guards. Once outside on the platform a cold wind slaps at him.

Victor has waited for him there, wired by mutual friends in Lausanne. Bleary, a little curt because he isn't quite awake yet, Victor hunches close to him. *Simon,* he says, *tell me what the hell are you doing? How do you think you can go back in there now?* He still clutches the telegram in his hand, waving it as if it were damning evidence. He tells Simon what their friends have wired to him—what they hadn't yet broken to Simon themselves before he slipped away. *Your brother and father,* he says with a shrug of his shoulders, *they are in a camp already—there is nothing to do but go back to Lausanne and wait. You can sit mourning for them there.*

How do I sit shiva if they are still alive? Simon demands irritably.

Victor eyes him quickly, and continues as if he hasn't heard. *We are here and we can do nothing, any of us, except wait.*

Together they stroll along the platform to an old Italian woman who is selling coffee and hard rolls. Little remains for either of them to say. Simon has known Victor since they were boys, and this is the first time they have ever stood, the two of them alone, and pretended to be friendly. As always, even in this new country, Victor is trim and so well groomed for the early morning that Simon can smell soap and lavender.

Come along—stay with me tonight before you go back, Victor offers.

Simon smiles and slips a coin into the old woman's dirty hand for both the coffees and shakes his head.

Eight people share the compartment as they head away from Zurich and back into the eastern mountains. It's not so cold anymore with all these bodies. Tired, hungry, Simon hasn't been able to sleep, but it's not really his brother or father he is thinking of. After all, they had their business to run and they wouldn't leave with him before and they even look alike. But his mother— he sees her clearly enough, her wandering blue eye and the other one that was always smiling for him. *I am glad you are dead first*, he thinks, ashamed of the thought and a little proud of it too, and afraid to wonder whether he'd really have gone past Zurich if Victor hadn't stopped him. Each jolt of the train jars him from his teeth to his stomach to his loins to his soul.

✳

The brandy burned pleasantly, well suited to the darkness and wind outside. Rachel had slowly, carefully, quite absently, frayed the rim of her paper cup with her fingers. Suddenly she glanced up at him again. Reaching across, she brushed his knee with her hand.

"How can we tell Mickie it's all right—that it doesn't matter?" she asked. She smiled at him, not so earnestly, almost shyly, as if the impossibility of such a thing were only too obvious.

"Does it matter that very much?" Simon said. He felt old and very distant from this woman his wife, and her playful smile annoyed him.

"No," she said, "it doesn't matter very much that she is a silly girl who never grows up or that she announces out of the blue that she's about to marry this one. Why not the Black boy she decided on last year without bothering to let him know? But Simon, can we bless her for it?"

"*I* can bless her for it."

"You can't," she snapped softly. "Not even if you wanted to—not after all we've done so she can be a Jew."

"We did all we did in Israel, and after it all we had won, and you said we couldn't stay. So here we are. Your granddaughter could have been a Jew in Israel."

Why do I do this? he wondered as tears gathered in her eyes, Rachel biting her lip, angry and hurt and determined. What might have been a thin drum of skin between them had split, tearing against itself as he watched, fascinated, a sinking in his stomach and bowels, but oddly enough without any pain at all.

The brandy was gone after a second portion for them both. Simon looked out the window, at his wife, out the window again, watching distantly, only mildly curious, as if this were all played out before him, beyond his reach or caring.

✳

The guard dozes in the bristling heat of the coach, rifle stiff as an afterthought between his knees. Now that he's asleep Simon can watch him. He feels little urgency or anticipation, simply a dull curiosity to see what will happen. Waiting has become easier over the long years, a habit.

Sweat soaks his shirt and jacket. It stings in his eyes with dust from the train and the desert, and his thighs are damp too. On every one of the first ten days of June he's made this same trip, riding in a different coach each time. No one has ever paid any attention to him.

They are running even later than usual today, he notes glumly through the window. The scrub and late-afternoon light of the desert are hard to read and, squinting, he tries to gauge how much longer it will take to reach the designated spot. The cheap pocket watch they have given him shows twelve minutes before seven. Another twelve minutes and it will be too late—the others, the ones waiting in the truck won't risk staying in the open. Simon's jaw clenches tight.

There—he cranes his neck out the window, pushing the wet hair back from his eyes—*there*, the long slow swell of an embankment arches towards the town, and the engine slows with the grade. First Simon closes his eyes and takes a deep breath. And in one quick motion he rises, pulls the wrench from his coat, and broods for an instant over the guard. For three years and more he's waited to fight someone, and here this man is snoring on, his nose running slightly, his skin soft and dark and very grimy too. Anger flushes through Simon, a rage that sickens him with blood pounding in his ears and throat and has nothing in the world to do with this body before him. Simon has no gun (in his squad there are so far only two pistols and a handful of grenades) not until he slams the wrench down and jerks the rifle out from between the guard's knees. Someone in another car has already pulled the emergency cord. And now Simon is yelling as the train grinds short—he yells and yells again, shoving and dragging the amazed, frozen passengers from their seats, from the posts they cling to.

Out! he cries, pleads. *Damn you*, he shouts at one boy, jabbing him clumsily in the ribs with the rifle. *Out, damn you, out.*

As the train slows he pushes one of them after another off into the sand and down the embankment, many of them tumbling head over heels. Already eight other members of his team are struggling up the hill towards the train, catching at the scrub so they can set dynamite charges stolen from the British.

A dizzy lightness sweeps up on Simon as he stands hanging

onto a rail by the open door of the carriage. His sweat has turned cold. The gun is very heavy. He swings it from the cold barrel, once and again and hurls it down the hill, butt first into the sand. The guard is heavier, slouching into his seat. Blood creeps over his ear and along his jaw. Lifting him isn't easy. Simon tries by the arms but can't manage any leverage. With little time for politeness, he grabs the man's feet and drags, heaves, as slowly the body flows, falling onto the floor and then into the sand below the track bed.

Racing for the truck with his team, Simon is streaked with sand and dust and grime from head to foot. He's too dry to sweat anymore. The new rifle, a pistol from another guard, fewer cartridges than they'd hoped—all are in the truck, the other men cleaning them already with rags and fingers. The dead, jarring, almost noiseless thumps of dynamite ring through the ground more than through the air, ringing perhaps with other trains and other charges set at this moment by teams across the Mandate. Once, twice, a third fails to come—they grimace in dismay—all muffled by the truck's whine and their laborious haste. They listen for each crack, swell, and the new silence, glancing at each other silently, wearing tight smiles.

Relieved more than anything else except frightened, afraid to move because he may shiver again and not be able to stop, Simon huddles in a corner of the truck, his knees drawn up outside the circle of faces. He wants only to be back in Petah Tikvah where Rachel will have soup for him. Israeli, she will ask nothing. But that boy of hers, that Eric (fifteen, too smart, son of a doctor who long ago caught himself in a crossfire of British, Arabs, Jews, or thieves), that boy will stare at Simon and not even wonder. Serene and smug, Eric has annoyed him from the beginning; they pantomime civility only for Rachel's sake. For the success of their first action, for the British train, for the man he hurt, Simon feels nothing, not even curiosity anymore.

✴

"How could we stay?" Rachel asked with a gentler tone. She patted out a wrinkle in her skirt. "That's so long ago," quietly to herself, "can it be so long?" Rousing herself slightly she leaned forward. "Why are you being this way? You know we had to leave, Simon—there was too much blood to stay."

He saw in his wife's eyes all the insistence of a reason for something which had never needed one before. When she'd washed dead men and cut their hair and tucked them in their shrouds, to earn a little money, a few vegetables while he was fighting—more often hiding—something like that look was in her eyes. And when they'd had their chance to leave after the independence, she'd had that same stare of inspired and absolute conviction he hadn't dared challenge.

Through the window he caught flashes of shadows and trees and dark fields quicksilver in moonlight, all come and gone in the lulling and violent pace of the train. *So, you are very beautiful,* he thought as he watched silently. *But then, you are young—the blood has drained from you so easily.*

Another long while had passed, it seemed, when he tore away from the window with a guilty jerk. Rachel looked weary. Pale in the dusk of the compartment, she sat facing him, sad and stubborn, not fiery anymore but still dogged. She looked old.

Simon glanced away again. Tired, heavy-limbed, not at all sleepy, he felt old too. And he was a little sad, a little scared, because he'd never really believed such a thing before. As if all those times he'd claimed the dues of age, the groans and the wisdom, had been a delicate front, a way of guarding the little, daring, secret lie that he wasn't really old at all.

"Little goose," he murmured awkwardly. He reached across and took her hand once more. She squeezed his fingers and smiled softly, distantly, before drawing back. For their dinner in town she'd worn a light touch of lip rouge. Now, though, only faint streaks of color remained on her grey lips.

Stubbornly, her head cocked to one side, she caught at the thread of the puzzle again without looking at him. "What did you fight for all those years—why did you fight?" she asked. "So your children and grandchildren cannot be Jews?"

"Myself, I'm not such a very good Jew," he said with a shrug.

Rachel turned her face to him with a haughty sneer. "For your Germans you were Jew enough. At least you don't run away from the truth."

"There is little enough to run from anymore."

"For heavens sake, that's what your granddaughter is doing. If she sees it or not doesn't matter. All we did—fought for, survived for—Mickie's denying it all."

"Her name is Rachel, and she doesn't mean it that way. She's only in love again. The last thing she means is to hurt us."

"What did you fight for, Simon?" Rachel, his wife, repeated.

"For nothing," he snapped, sharp and quick, his voice cracking. But suddenly his face brightened as he discovered a new secret. "No, that's not right. You know the real truth?—I fought only so I could fight at last. Isn't that simple? Isn't that fine? There never was any *reason*."

Angrily she waved this off. "It's a fine time for you to say this only now."

He smiled a joyless smile. "You make your reasons for thirty years ago—I do too. Where does it get us?"

Once more she began, speaking slowly to explain a simple mystery. "I am a Jew, yes? Eric I raised to be a Jew." Hesitating for an instant, she met his eyes. He nodded, wearing the same smile, though a little grimmer, almost taunting. "He is not your son—you never wanted that." (Simon remembered Eric's ancient disdain, his smugness now that he was a well-to-do obstetrician, and thanked the heavens she was right). "But Rachel is your granddaughter, so you say. And she will hurt her father—and me."

A hot flush of color reached into her cheeks, and he checked his smile because it would show the triumph he felt, guilty and giddy and ashamed of it. "What did I fight for?" he asked very quietly. "To give her such a choice."

The cadence of the tracks was numbing, endless. They rolled as it rocked them, so that for a while they could hear nothing else, could not even hear it, only silence.

Simon rubbed his eyes, well aware that nothing had changed after all. Their talk finally meant nothing—all that mattered was what would come in Chicago. That's what had scared him from the start. *You always come right to the point*, he snorted at himself, and his wife glanced up.

"She isn't dead, you know," he said. "You can't sit *shiva* for her if all she's done is marry that boy."

Rachel sat quietly staring at him, amazed—as if he'd lost his mind—and she smiled. (Simon thought it was a terrible smile.) "Of course not. Why would I ever do that?" she said, she the triumphant one now. "Do you think I would pretend to go into mourning for her—here, in America? How silly that would be. It wouldn't mean a thing here. You don't give me enough credit, Simon."

"Maybe not," he said. "So what are you going to do?"

"I won't *do* anything. What can I do? The girl and this husband of hers, whoever he is, won't be welcome in my house. Not if she goes ahead with this." Her voice was flat and hard, her eyes bright. "She hurts my Eric, she betrays us, and I will not bless her for it."

With each jar of the train Simon fell farther and farther away, helplessly watching this woman from very far away. "I will visit her if she wishes," he said too loudly.

Rachel shrugged. They'd triumphed, each of them now. The night was late, and she rose at last to prepare for bed. Simon did not look up. On the day of independence it had been a very late night too and he hadn't been with her. That was maybe the last time.

They were silent—she did not call him to bed, and he stared at the window. The moon was hidden or had gone down. He could see only the night and shadows and a faint distorting reflection of their compartment. It was very dark for the few hours before dawn, and he wanted to wait for it. But the train coaxed and rocked him, rushing and swaying, the tracks singing, and he was tired.

Carnegie Mellon Series in Short Fiction

Sharon Dilworth, Editor

Lynne Barrett
    The Land of Go
    The Secret Names of Women

Michelle Herman
    A New and Glorious Life

David Lynn
    Fortune Telling

Pamela Painter
    The Long and Short of It

Eve Shelnutt
    The Girl, Painted